A JOLLY LITTLE SCANDAL

(SENSUAL SCANDALS - PREQUEL 0.5)

TABETHA WAITE

Cover Design by The Midnight Muse

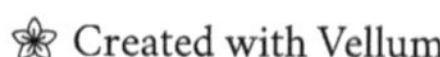

ALSO BY TABETHA WAITE

Also by Tabetha Waite

Ways of Love Historical Romance Series

How it All Began for the Baron (Christmas prequel novella)

Why the Earl is After the Girl (Book 1)

Where the Viscount Met His Match (Book 2)

When a Duke Pursues a Lady (Book 3)

Who the Marquess Dares to Desire (Book 4)

What a Gentleman Does for Love (Book 5)

Season of the Spinster Series

Triana's Spring Seduction (Book 1)

Isabella's Secret Summer (Book 2)

The Spinster's Alluring Season (Book 2.5)

Alyssa's Autumn Affair (Book 3)

Korina's Wild Winter (Book 4)

Wanton Wastrels

The Rapscallion's Romance

The Marauder's Mistress

Sensual Scandals

A Jolly Little Scandal (0.5 prequel)

Novellas

The Harlot's Hero

Frozen Fancy

Novels

Behind a Moonlit Veil

The Secrets of Shadows

The Piper's Paramour

Kiernan Fantasy Series

The Kingdoms of Kiernan (Kiernan – Book 1)

Collections

An Everlasting Amour (A collection of short stories)

An Everlasting Christmas Amour

An Everlasting Regency Amour

An Everlasting Regency Amour – Volume 2

The Wedding Wager

The Brazen Belles Anthology

Heyer Society (non-fiction essays)

For Dawn Brower who invited me to join the original "Christmas on Scandal Lane" anthology set which turned into a brand new series! Something so simple got the wheels of imagination turning for the Bevelstroke sisters!

CHAPTER 1

London, England
December 1823

"IT APPEARS that we're causing quite a stir, ladies," Miss Araminta Bevelstroke said sarcastically as she took a seat in the Duke of Marlington's private box at the Theatre Royal. Although, with the recent death of her half-sisters' shared sire, she supposed it now belonged to them.

She lifted her opera glasses to her gray eyes and surveyed the assemblage with a twitch of her lips. She could feel the haughty stares on them, telling them that they didn't belong, but she didn't really care because honestly… they did. Their blood was as blue as any single one of the ladies here, gossiping behind their twittering fans. The only difference was that they had chosen to move to London and live together under one roof at number twenty-five Grosvenor Square without a "proper" chaperone.

"We are the latest novelty, Minty." Isadora's dry voice came from next to her. She was the eldest of the Bevelstroke sisters at eight and twenty. "Four sisters with different mothers who have found means in which to live independently without the ties of marriage? Why, the drawing rooms are a veritable beehive of activity that we should prefer this sort of meaningless existence." Her lips lifted at the corners. "We will be creating a stir for some time, I imagine."

"I agree with Isa," Calliope tossed her red hair and added to the conversation from where she sat behind her two elder siblings. "Since this is our first public outing, we'll likely be in the papers tomorrow, even though we moved in just yesterday afternoon." She turned to the quiet blond woman at her side who had yet to voice an opinion. Olivia was the youngest of the Bevelstroke women. At only eighteen years of age, she was barely out of the schoolroom. "Surely you have an opinion, Livy?"

The girl shrugged. "Not particularly—"

Araminta waved a hand and interjected, "The excitement will die down soon enough, once another scandal arises to take its place. I daresay it won't be long before some unsuspecting heiress is tempted by a charming gentleman to travel down the road to ruin on Scandal Lane."

"Ah, yes. Scandal Lane," Isadora murmured. "Many women have been brought down by that notorious path in Hyde Park."

"Then perhaps we should take a stroll there some afternoon and see what all the fuss is about," Calliope suggested, as she leaned forward with a wicked gleam in her gaze.

Araminta rolled her eyes, for their red-haired sister had always been rather daring when it came to... well, just about anything. She had been the hoyden who had tucked her skirts into her waist and climbed trees with a daring display of more than just her ankles. Entire legs had been visible and her exploits had caught the attention of several of the village boys, much to their father's dismay.

But if there was one thing the Duke of Marlington was known for, it was the love and patience he'd had for all four of his daughters. He had gracefully ignored the fact that he was known as the Black Widower with the deaths of four wives from various ailments.

Isadora's mother had been the first duchess, and although she had been an accomplished horsewoman, she had died of a broken neck in a fall from her favorite mount when her daughter was just a year old.

Araminta's mother was next. She died of a fever the year Araminta turned three, but she was told her mother's health had always been rather frail.

Next, came Calliope. Her mother left the earth when Calliope was six months old after suffering from a weak heart following her birth.

Olivia's mother didn't even live long enough to see her daughter, for she perished on the birthing bed.

After mourning four wives, the duke decided that he was through trying to beget an heir and that he wished to spend the rest of his life in peace with his beloved girls. He became a devoted father and never pressured them into marriage like many men of the aristocracy were wont to do. In the face of such grief, he had been rather lenient with their upbringing, some would claim too much so, and encouraged them to find their own way, even if marriage wasn't part of the bargain.

Granted, he had employed a governess, although the sisters never went away to school, the duke choosing to teach them how to run a proper estate instead. As if they were the true heirs that would take over upon his demise, which they all knew would be impossible since it had to be a male. While Araminta had never been certain who would take over the dukedom after their father's passing, she prayed it would be someone who would take care of the tenants' needs, just as their sire had.

When their father had died the previous summer, Araminta and her sisters had wept for days, his acute loss felt by all of them. Six months later, when they had come out of mourning, his will had been read by the London solicitor. He told them that the duke had saved each of their mother's dowries for their personal use and bequeathed the townhouse in London to them, which wasn't entailed, so they had begun to pack up their things to begin a new life, each vowing that they would honor their father's memory by continuing to be the independent women he'd taught them to be.

Araminta glanced down at her bright red satin gown and decided that this display of rebellion was her first act as a six and twenty-year-old self-reliant woman of the *ton.* She would love to have the chance to be a role model to other women who wished for the same sort of individualism. And she intended to start an afternoon tea for like-minded ladies for just that purpose at the earliest opportunity.

With that goal in mind, she sat back in her seat and settled in to enjoy the rest of the play.

~

GREYSON HARTFIELD, the Earl of Somers, narrowed his eyes as he turned to the gentleman next to him. "Do you think the rumors are true, that those women are Marlington's daughters?"

Sebastian didn't even lift his head where it was laid back against his seat, although he did open an eye and peer back at his companion through a slit lid. "I can't really say since I was enjoying a bit of relaxation until I was interrupted."

Grey rolled his eyes and muttered, "I don't know why you bother attending the theatre if all you do is sleep through the performance."

Seb just shrugged his shoulders and said, "I come because I enjoy the flirtations to be had during intermission—" He paused with a decided tilt to his mouth. "Although backstage is where the real fun happens."

"I have no doubt you know each actress *personally.*"

This time Seb opened both of his eyes. "And what's wrong with that?" He frowned slightly. "It's not as if you haven't sampled the delights to be had from time to time."

Indeed, Grey himself had certainly enjoyed his share of sexual exploits for most of his three and thirty years, but he was starting to find it all rather… unsatisfying. His expression turned somber. "Perhaps it's time I settled down."

His announcement surprised him as much as it had Sebastian Ford, Viscount Blakely. Grey had first met Seb in Eton and since then, they had been good friends. There was no one he would trust more with his life, although when Grey's sister had made her come out ten years before, he'd made sure Seb was nowhere around her. Females were a completely different story, for he knew too much of the viscount's history. In truth, it rather mirrored his own. But while Grey was actually finding it time to think of doing his duty to his familial line, Seb could care less.

"Are you mad?" Blakely stared at him as if he might jump over the box and leap to his death at any moment. "Surely you can't be serious about setting up a nursery. Haven't you enough nieces and nephews to keep you occupied?"

It was true that Grey's sister had made their mother rather proud by giving birth to her ninth child just a fortnight ago. In truth, ever since she'd said her vows and married Eli Seaton, Viscount Montrose, her belly had been swollen each time he'd paid a call, but it was the brilliant smile on her still youthful face that he hadn't quite been able to forget.

Grey looked back across the expanse to where the brunette in the red dress was sitting with her sisters and murmured, "Things change, Seb." He tore his eyes away and returned them to Blakely. "And what would make my mother more thrilled than a Christmas proposal?"

Sebastian blinked in horror. "That's only three weeks away! My God, you *have* lost your senses. I believe an intervention is in order. Perhaps I should summon a physician—"

"Oh, stuff it," Grey snapped, although the smirk belied the annoyance he wished to convey. "The only thing I need is an *introduction* to the lady in red."

Sebastian finally appeared interested enough to sit forward and take a pair of opera glasses to inspect the box situated across from them. After a moment he said, "I suppose she's a comely enough chit, but for the rest of your days?" He shuddered. "Heaven help me if I'm saddled with only one woman day in and day out. The constant nagging would be enough to send me to an early grave." He lowered the glasses. "If you are serious about this quest then I would suggest having your tailor expand the waist bands on your trousers."

Grey chose to hold his tongue as Seb put the glasses back up to his eyes. "Oh, now that's interesting."

"What is?" Grey asked dryly, almost dreading to hear the answer.

He expected Sebastian to note how when the lady in red smiled it was a bit "toothy," or some such nonsense, but instead, he murmured, "I didn't know Marlington sired a *red-haired* gel." He lowered the glasses a second time and flashed him a wicked grin. "Indeed. You are quite right about those introductions."

Grey snorted, although he knew that flame haired ladies were one of Seb's few weaknesses when it came to the fairer sex. He seldom resisted the urge to bed a woman who sported those copper locks. "I would prefer to make a good impression, so if we get the opportunity to meet them, perhaps you might curtail your urges for a time."

"What a killjoy you're turning out to be, and rather surly in your dotage," Seb returned sourly. But he heaved a sigh. "Fine. I'll give you to Christmas before I engage her services."

Grey shook his head, but he agreed. "I appreciate that, Blakely. Now the question is, who do we know who can assist us in making their acquaintance?"

Seb seemed to ponder this for a moment, and then said, "I may be able to help with that."

~

"THOSE GENTLEMAN ARE RATHER UNNERVING." Araminta glanced at Isadora, who was scanning the box across from them with a critical eye. "They keep staring at us."

"Who wouldn't?" Araminta said with a smirk. "Honestly, Isa, put those things down and watch the play. We will deal with the mob at intermission."

Isadora reluctantly set the glasses aside. "I merely feel it is my responsibility, as the eldest sister, to watch out for the rest of you."

Araminta took her hand. "Isa, the whole purpose of this endeavor in London is to be independent. That doesn't mean you have to assume the role of chaperone. We vowed to make our own decisions, no matter the consequences. Father always told us that the only way we shall learn is to forgive our mistakes. How shall we do that if you choose to flutter about like a mother hen?"

Isadora frowned, but she seemed to be contemplating her words.

"Besides," Araminta added with a shrug. "What's the harm in a bit of flirtation?

We are intending to join society, are we not? We shall have to learn how to survive the dangerous waters of the *ton*. You won't be there to protect us all of the time."

"I see no reason to unnecessarily tempt fate either," Isa pointed out. "We didn't come here to be ridiculed and shunned by our peers. We wanted to prove that we could survive without marriage."

"And we shall," Araminta agreed firmly. She lowered her voice as her eyes shifted to their younger sisters sitting behind them.

"Although I worry so about Livy. She has never been quite as outspoken as the rest of us. I fear for her future if something should happen to us. I think we should encourage a proper match for her."

Isa nodded. "I think you're right. But what about Calliope?"

Araminta rolled her eyes. "That girl has more spirit than you and I combined. The only thing I should be concerned with her is the trail of broken hearts she will leave across London."

Her elder sister laughed, knowing that it was true. Callie was like a kite flowing away on the breeze, completely without restraint. If any gentleman managed to tie her down, it would be nothing short of a miracle.

As intermission came upon them, it didn't take long before their box was filled with curious spectators of society, matrons eager to meet the secretive Marlington sisters who had spent very little time in the city. Under the guise of paying their respects to a man they had barely even known, Araminta found that it didn't take much for them to start peppering them with questions. When it became clear that they were living under one roof without a chaperone, several eyebrows lifted to their hairline in surprise and more than a touch of censure.

"Surely there is an aged aunt who might assist you," one lady suggested.

"On the contrary," Araminta pointed out proudly. "We are quite content with our current situation. Besides, it's not as if my sister and I are fresh out of the schoolroom."

"Indeed, not." The lady had huffed indignantly. "But I'm not sure being a spinster is something I should be proud of."

Araminta merely smiled. "I choose to consider it as self-reliance." She lifted a brow. "Or perhaps freedom from enslavement."

She took a bit of pleasure in seeing the woman's mouth drop open before she flounced out of the box with a decided huff.

"Making friends already, I see," Isadora drawled from beside her.

"I have a particular talent for chasing away the unwanted," Araminta said proudly.

Her sister merely snorted in return.

Araminta was still wearing a smile when she glanced toward the back of the box where the crowd had thinned. But it slipped slightly, her heart picking up speed when she spied a tall man ducking to enter. He was quite breathtaking with his pitch-black hair and shocking blue eyes that seemed to take in more than his expression would ever reveal. He was dressed in the height of fashion, in stark black and white, but she decided that made him appear even more appealing than if he was decked out in color like a dandy.

Their eyes clashed and she quickly looked away, something that rather shocked her, for she was usually the stronger one. As her gaze shifted to the man at his side, equally appealing with his shock of blond hair and dark eyes that held a wicked gleam in their depths, he didn't affect her nearly as much as the first.

A woman, whom Araminta had completely overlooked until that point, walked forward and offered a slight curtsy, which Araminta returned. "Good evening. I was tasked with making introductions." She turned to Isa. "Lady Isadora. It's a pleasure to see you again."

"Lady Abaline," Isadora returned evenly. "I didn't realize you would be in town so soon after your husband's death. Allow me to offer my condolences."

"Thank you." The other woman's smile was rather tight, although she returned with a challenge in her tone, "But then, you're not the only one who can defy convention, are you?"

"Apparently not," Isa murmured. She turned to Araminta. "Surely you remember the former Miss Sabine Groves? She wed our neighbor in Broxbourne, the Baron Abaline a year ago, but the union was decidedly short. Was it even a month?"

Memory finally surfaced in Araminta's brain. From what she could remember of the baron, he had been a kindly, grandfather sort of figure who had grown children. He had visited her father several times over the years. But why he'd felt the need to marry such a girl as Sabine when he could have spent his last days in peace was beyond her comprehension.

"Indeed, accidents happen all the time." Lady Abaline blinked innocently. "From what I understand, your father knew that all too well."

When Isadora opened her mouth to reply to such a nasty comment, Araminta realized that it was time to intercede before a brawl ensued. While Isadora might not have trained with Gentleman Jackson in London, she had been taught how to deliver a rather effective punch to the jaw. Their father had told her it was one of her best traits.

"Perhaps now isn't the time—"

"Lady Abaline, if you could cease—"

Araminta stopped midsentence, as did the dark-haired man who had stepped forward at the same time with his own plea for a cease-fire.

Without even waiting for the baroness to reply, he bowed politely to Araminta. "Forgive the intrusion, my lady. My friend and I were merely wishing to gain an audience properly." He leveled a glare at the blond gentleman. "I see now that was a mistake and we should have just prevailed upon your good graces." He gestured to Lady Abaline, who was then taken by the arm and escorted out of the box by his companion.

Once they were gone, he returned his attention to her. "Allow me to introduce myself if I may. I'm Greyson Hartfield, the Earl of Somers. And you are?"

He waited patiently for her to supply her name, which she did. "Lady Araminta Bevelstroke, my lord. And these are my sisters, Lady Isadora, Lady Calliope, and Lady Olivia."

He inclined his head to each one in turn and Araminta was glad to see that the set of Isadora's shoulders had relaxed slightly, the tension in her frame dissipating somewhat with Lady

Abaline's departure and the ensuing charm from Lord Somers. "Dare I hope to see you ladies about town more often?"

That blue gaze shifted to Araminta and held, as if he was addressing her in particular. For some inane reason, her heart thumped erratically at the idea. "You can guarantee it, my lord."

CHAPTER 2

"Wonderful idea, enlisting the help of one of your former paramours to make a good impression on the Marlington chits." Grey smacked his gloves on his thigh, the light snow falling outside still clinging to his greatcoat, as he glared at Seb across from him in his carriage. His friend had joined him at the theatre that evening, although after what had taken place, Grey nearly left him there to take a hackney home.

"How was I to know that they knew each other and didn't get along?" Seb grumbled, his arms folded across his chest. "As if I'm pleased about this unfortunate set of circumstances either. The actress I had my eye on wouldn't even grant me a private audience after she saw me trying to placate Lady Abaline."

"How dreadful," Grey said with disinterest.

Sebastian leveled a glare at him. "I'm not sure you're going to get very far with Lady Araminta even if I'd had nothing to do with it. Something tells she isn't going to be as easy for you to win over as you might think."

"You forget that my intentions are *honorable*," he pointed out. "Unlike your designs on Lady Calliope."

Seb continued to adopt a surly demeanor. "The chit wouldn't even deign to look at me. Then again—" He rubbed his chin thoughtfully. "I've never been one to shirk a challenge." He sat up straighter. "Where did you say they would be next?"

Grey glared at him. "They didn't." He sighed heavily. "Again, let me remind you that I would like to try and gain the lady's favor."

"Odd's fish, Grey." Sebastian rested a foot on the opposite side of the carriage. "You make me sound as if I'm going to start humping the gel's leg in the middle of a ballroom."

Grey merely lifted a brow. "Is that really so farfetched?" He interlaced his hands over his taut stomach. "Tell me again how many ladies you've courted down Scandal Lane."

Blakely held up a finger. "*None* that didn't wish to be led down that path, I assure you." He suddenly frowned. "To be honest, I don't think you're upset with me so much as yourself."

"And why would that be?" Grey asked tolerantly, not particularly in the mood to humor his longtime friend, but finding that he was doing it anyway.

"You are just like me, used to getting what you want from all sorts of willing women, and yet, when it comes to imparting the same sort of experience that you've gained through the years, it failed to impress and it's bothering you." He leaned back as if he'd signified the conclusion of their conversation when Grey wasn't nearly done.

He leaned forward and settled his elbows on his knees. "So let me get this right. You think I'm upset with you because of some sort of misguided sense of pride that was bruised on my behalf?"

Seb spread his arms wide. "I rest my case."

Grey laughed. "That's because there *is* no argument!" he countered, and then shook his head. "But seeing as how this will undoubtedly turn into a useless altercation, I'm going to sit here and hold my tongue until I get home where I will have a long, soothing drink of brandy before I decide the best way to win this fair maiden's heart."

As if on cue, the carriage rolled to a stop before White's, where Sebastian took his leave. However, before he departed, he leaned back in the carriage and said, "While I'm sure you don't want any more of my adoring advice, my suggestion is to find another 'fair maiden,' because I don't think you're going to convince Lady Araminta of your sincerity, especially once your reputation as a rake reaches her ears."

With that, he slapped his hand on the carriage, not only to add credence to his statement, but also to let the driver know his master was ready to depart.

As the carriage pulled away from the curb, Grey mulled over the viscount's words. Sebastian might be a libertine in the most torrid of definitions, but the man also knew how to read women. If he imagined she would be difficult to court, then he was more than likely right.

He tapped a finger on his thigh in contemplation. So if this wasn't to be a conventional courtship with roses and flowery prose, he had to figure out what the lady loved best.

Only then would his plan to secure Lady Araminta as his wife succeed.

~

"THE INVITATIONS, MY LADY." The butler bowed reverently to Araminta as he held out a silver tray.

"Ooh! Already?" Calliope nearly jumped up and down in her chair with excitement while Olivia barely even glanced up from the novel she was reading. Isadora wasn't even in the room, but Araminta guessed she was likely outdoors somewhere taking a brisk walk. She had always enjoyed the exercise and preferred the quiet beauty of nature to an indoor parlor, even if it was snowing rather steadily at the moment.

"Patience, Callie," she admonished her younger sibling. She lifted the pile of folded parchment from the tray and sifted through the various seals. Most, she noted, were invitations to afternoon tea, likely so they could be scrutinized more thoroughly than they had been at the theatre. But when she came across one that held a ducal seal, she found herself intrigued and opened it.

She must have been taking too long to read it, for Calliope nearly burst from her chair, "Well? What is it?"

"It's an invitation to a Christmas Eve ball next Saturday."

Calliope clapped her hands together. "Oh, how delightful! I know just what to wear!"

Araminta noticed that Olivia didn't share in her sister's excitement. "What about you, Livy? It's about time we put some of those dancing lessons to use, isn't it?"

She shrugged one shoulder, but didn't lift her green gaze, keeping it glued to the page she had been on for the past quarter hour. "I'd much rather stay in. I'm not that eager to venture out in the cold."

Araminta knew that Olivia had always hated winter, and generally asked to stay back when her sisters would choose to go out and play in the snow. "I know that, dearest, but perhaps you could make an exception for the holiday season for us? Besides, it would be best if we continued to adapt a united front for society."

She tried to adopt a hopeful note to her voice and it worked for the youngest Bevelstroke sister sighed heavily and said, "Very well."

"Splendid!" Calliope cheered.

"What's so splendid?" Isadora said dryly as she walked in, the evidence of the falling snow still visible in her dark hair. As the eldest she was generally content to allow Araminta to act as though she was the leader of their small pack, but Araminta still found it necessary to gain her approval on most matters as a show of respect.

"We've been invited to a Christmas Eve ball by the Duchess of Gravesend." She handed the item in question to Isa, who flicked her gaze across the elegant penmanship and then handed it back to her.

"I suppose we're going?" she asked.

Araminta didn't even get a chance to reply before Calliope was chiming in with, "Yes! Isn't it grand? I've always dreamed of spending the Christmas season in London! I daresay I'm going to enjoy Bond Street to its fullest, and I intend to buy gifts for all of you and perhaps even a few for myself."

"You might want to curb some of those spending habits," Isadora noted. "Or else reconsider your aversion to marriage. Only a wealthy lord will be able to keep you happy if you are determined to be outfitted in the latest fashions."

This instantly caused Calliope to scrunch up her nose in distaste. "Father assured us that we were provided for and I would hardly call my inheritance of five thousand pounds that of a pauper. What does it matter if I choose to indulge now and then?"

"Because you seem to "indulge" quite often," Isadora countered.

Calliope gave an indignant sniff and stood. "Be that as it may, I will return shortly with a new bonnet. Or perhaps *two*."

She nearly stomped out the door, her defiance causing Araminta to shake her head. "Do you really think anyone would marry her?" she asked Isadora.

"I wouldn't," Olivia piped up from where she sat; although now she got to her feet—book still firmly in hand. "If you'll excuse me, I'm going to the library where I can actually concentrate."

Isadora turned her silver eyes on Araminta. "I feel as though I broke up a party."

"Not to worry," she replied. "You've lived with us long enough you should know our personalities clash now and again. In truth, if we weren't sisters, sometimes I wonder if we would even like each other."

Isa laughed at that. "I was thinking the exact same thing."

~

SHORTLY THEREAFTER, Isadora went to her room to take a nap, so that left Araminta with some time on her own. Since it was early afternoon, she decided to take her horse out for a ride in the park. She had always enjoyed riding as a child, and what a perfect opportunity as it would give her to chance to see and be seen on the infamous Rotten Row.

She headed to her room and rang for her maid to assist her into a deep purple, velvet riding habit and after settling her matching bonnet on her brown hair and pulling on her leather gloves, she grabbed her riding crop and headed to the stables behind the house. Most of their servants had been employed at the duke's estate, but had chosen to move to London with them, the groom included.

"Good day, Magnus," she greeted the older man with his shock of white hair with a wide smile. He was brushing down Calliope's mare when she arrived. "I was hoping you might saddle Destiny for me?"

He returned her greeting. "I'd be glad to, my lady." He set down the brush on the stall door and after giving the mare an affectionate pat on the neck, he left the pen and grabbed a sidesaddle and began to talk gently to the chestnut mare with the white stripe on her nose. It was his easy manner and patience with the horses that had made Araminta coerce him to join them in the city, even though he had preferred the simplicity of the country. He also didn't question her sanity when she chose to go riding in all sorts of weather.

She lifted her face to the sky and smiled as the snow softly landed on her face and eyelashes, enveloping everything around her in a blanket of white. "It's a lovely day isn't it?" She'd always loved the silence back at the estate, but in London, there wasn't much that remained still for long.

"I'm not so sure about that, my lady," he countered. "While I might like a bit of snow, I'm afraid my old bones don't much care for it. But that's part of the aging process I suppose."

"It's certainly better than the alternative. I daresay I don't know what I'd do without you." She winked at him and he chuckled as he led out the mare.

"I appreciate that, my lady. I enjoyed working for the duke and his daughters were no exception."

As the horse caught the scent of her mistress, she tossed her head with a snort. Araminta removed one of her gloves and rubbed her hand along the velvety nose. The horse's nostrils flared, absorbing her scent as Araminta cooed softly to her. She led her over to the mounting block and set her left foot in the stirrup and then swung her right leg over the saddle horn.

Once Araminta was perched atop, she donned her glove once more, grabbed the reins and clucked her tongue at Destiny. She offered a farewell wave to Magnus as the mare instantly began to walk.

It was a brief ride to Hyde Park, which was situated just to the west of Grosvenor Square. As she passed through the gates, Araminta wasn't surprised to see that there were several people in fashionable attire milling about. It appeared that the peerage didn't allow a bit of snow to deter them from getting out either.

As she started to promenade along the path, she received more curious stares than actual acknowledgement, but she nevertheless kept her chin high and a smile on her face, inclining her head whenever she caught the direct gazes from various passerby and praying that her nose wasn't already the color of a ripe cherry, although it likely was. While much of the peerage preferred to remain at their estates throughout the winter, the holiday season was particularly festive and many returned to town to celebrate.

Araminta hadn't been riding long when she heard the approaching trot of another horse. She glanced to her left when someone paused to join her.

"I thought that might have been you, Lady Araminta."

For a moment, she was taken aback by the charming grin Lord Somers bestowed upon her, showing perfect white teeth. Not only that, but he cut quite a dashing figure with his layered greatcoat flying out behind him as he straddled a black stallion. With a hat sitting on his dark head and his piercing blue eyes flashing with the promise of mirth, he was rather handsome indeed.

"Good day, my lord." She cursed the breathless quality of her voice and prayed that he hadn't noticed as she turned her attention back to the road in front of her.

"Ouch," he murmured. "Did I make such a bad impression last night where that's all the greeting I should receive?"

Araminta laughed. "What would you expect me to say? We have just met, after all. I don't know anything about you."

"Fair point," he returned. She glanced to see that he was rubbing the side of his jaw. It was particularly distracting to her peace of mind, so she turned her head forward once more. "I should like to rectify that. What would you wish to know about me?"

She thought for a moment and said, "Do you have any family?"

"Indeed. While my father is gone, my mother is still alive to plague my days. I also have a sister, Melinda, who is happily married. At least it appears that way to me for she has nine children."

"*Nine*?" Araminta echoed, as she looked at him in surprise.

The set of his mouth was too enticing by half. "Surely having a family of your own someday is an aspiration you hold?"

"On the contrary," she returned, trying not to be too affected by the smooth, deep timbre of his voice. "My sisters and I are determined to live by independent means."

"And yet, you all live together," he pointed out.

"For now, yes," she admitted with a laugh. "But only until we decide what business venture we wish to embark on. It's convenient, for the moment, for us to stay at our father's former townhouse while we get our foothold in society. But eventually, we intend to go our separate ways."

He appeared skeptical. "So you're not hoping to join the marriage mart?"

She shook her head. "Not at all. However, you never know what business prospects you might uncover when you are dancing the waltz."

"I see."

Araminta wasn't sure if he sounded impressed or… something else. She just prayed it wasn't censure. She was quite sure they would have enough of that before the Christmas season was over.

GREY WAS RATHER disappointed to hear that the lady had no designs on marriage, when that was what he was hoping to gain from her. Ironically enough, he wasn't even sure why he'd suddenly set his sights on Lady Araminta Bevelstroke, pondering that fact much of the night before as he'd returned home. He decided it was merely that, of all the other ladies he'd met in London, he knew that life with her would never be boring. Just the short time he'd been in her company, he could tell she was a strong, intelligent woman. If the determined glint in her eye and her speech today hadn't proven that, as she'd sat at the theatre last night with complete confidence, her head held high, back straight, and shoulders square, it would have proven his theory. Combined with the fact she was rather comely, he imagined they could make a rather comfortable match together.

The issue he would undoubtedly face is trying to convince her of the same thing.

"So you have no desire to wed?" he prodded.

She laughed, the delightful sound going straight to his groin. "I don't know why people find that so difficult to believe. I am a woman, but that doesn't mean I can't make my own way. Several women in history have done just that. Look at Jane Austen."

He slanted a glance at her. "You do know that she wrote her novels anonymously."

"But—" She held up a hand. "She made sure to note that the author was a *lady* and in spite of her gender, she was quite successful."

"So your aspirations are to be a writer then?" he asked curiously.

She shrugged. "Honestly, I'm not sure yet. I said we're all still considering our options, but that is what is good about being independent. I don't have a husband telling me what I can or cannot do. As a single woman, I have the chance to let my voice be heard, instead of—" Her cheeks abruptly colored, likely from embarrassment, for Grey had a good idea of what she'd been about to say.

"Instead of wasting away with a brood of children?" he guessed and her face merely burned brighter.

"I didn't mean to infer anything derogatory toward your sister," she explained, and he noted that she appeared sincere. "She made her choice, and I have made mine. Our paths are just different."

Grey considered his next move, and then decided that if he wished to win over the lady, he would have to play by her rules. She might think that she didn't want to marry, but she obviously hadn't had the chance to be convinced otherwise.

He intended to change her mind.

With a slight smile curving his lips, he knew just what to do.

CHAPTER 3

"Livy? Are you ready, dearest?" Araminta knocked on her youngest sister's bedchamber door. "We're all waiting for you downstairs."

As Araminta waited for Olivia to answer her summons, her mind drifted back to Lord Somers. She'd had a rather nice time conversing with him that afternoon, and much of their interlude had been swirling through her mind after she'd returned home. In truth, she could have spent more time in his company, but she hadn't wanted to be late to their first social event at the widowed Countess of Everlake's home.

The door opened slightly, and Olivia stood there in a light green satin gown. She would have looked perfectly charming if her expression didn't match the color of her dress. Her jade eyes were wide and almost fearful. "Must I go?"

"Yes," Araminta said firmly. She knew that her sister preferred her fictional characters to those in real life, but she would never get past her nervousness if Araminta didn't shove her out of the house now and again. But seeing the dismay on Olivia's face still tore at her heart. She reached out and took her sister's cold hand in her own. "It's not as if you have to dance. It's to be a small gathering filled with parlor games. Doesn't that sound fun?" she cajoled. "I know how much you love to play Spillkins."

Olivia wavered for a moment and then sighed heavily. "Very well." She moved into the hall and Araminta considered that to be a victory, however small. She threaded Livy's arm through her own and together they descended the stairs.

As she caught Isa's eye, she could see the relief in her elder sister's gaze, while Calliope stopped her pacing and said in a huff, "Finally!"

As a united front, they gathered their wraps then walked to the carriage and climbed inside, doing their best to avoid the worst of the snowdrifts around them. After snowing quite heavily for most of the day, it looked like a winter wonderland and Araminta couldn't have been happier. Olivia, however, turned her focus outside to stare blankly at the darkness beyond. She still wasn't eager to attend the gathering, but at least she was in the coach.

Araminta smoothed her hands down the front of her ivory gown and then glanced at Isadora and Calliope seated across from her. Isa had chosen a sapphire blue dress to wear, and Araminta decided that it complimented her black hair rather nicely. In turn, Calliope had opted for a rose gown, which actually brought out the copper tints in her hair. Not many ladies would dare to wear pink with such coloring, but then, Araminta realized that there wasn't much Calliope couldn't get away with. And even then, she would likely defy convention to do it anyway.

As they arrived at the Everlakes' stately townhome with its large white columns, they alighted from the carriage with the assistance of a footman as they walked up the expansive steps.

Inside, Araminta could hear the buzz of activity and laughter coming from various rooms and as their hostess sailed over to greet them in a plum-colored dress with diamonds winking at her throat and ears, she said with a wide grin, "You must be the

Bevelstroke sisters, the toast of London this Christmas season. I'm Lady Everlake."

Araminta laughed and then offered a polite curtsy. "I'm not sure about that, my lady, but yes you are correct in that we are the daughters of the late Duke of Marlington. My name is Araminta, and this is Isadora, Calliope, and Olivia." She gestured to each of her sisters in turn, who nodded respectfully.

"It's lovely to have you here this evening," the countess remarked. She held up a hand, and a footman walked over to hand them each a sheet of parchment. "This is a guide to where the various games will be held. There will be refreshments on hand so you won't get parched." She offered a kind smile. "I do hope that you enjoy yourselves."

"I'm sure we will," Araminta returned. "Thank you for the invitation."

As the lady moved away to greet more guests that had arrived, she turned to her sisters who were perusing the various games. "I know where I shall go first," Calliope announced. "Charades!" With a slight squeak of excitement, she headed in that direction.

"I think I shall broaden my mind with some riddles." Isadora was the next to leave.

"I don't see Spillkins listed, Minty," Olivia said somewhat anxiously.

Araminta patted her arm. "Never you fret. I see board games listed in the front parlor, so perhaps we will get lucky in there."

LORD BLAKELY PULLED at his cravat in agitation. "Must we engage in such absolutely boring pursuits?" Seb nearly whined. "I have debased myself more often than not in the quest for a particular female, but this one truly tops the list."

Grey rolled his eyes. "I doubt this is the worst thing you've done by far. Either way, you might recall you are here as a favor to me. I was told this is where the Bevelstroke sisters would be this evening so here we are. Besides, I doubt it will be as awful as you imagine."

As their hostess walked forward, Grey shot his companion a warning look.

"Curse women and their red hair," Sebastian grumbled under his breath, although he adopted a perfectly charming grin, as if there wasn't anywhere else he'd rather be that evening than the Countess of Everlake's residence.

"Good evening, gentlemen." She greeted them with a broad smile. "I'm so glad you could make it."

"It's nice to get out of the gaming hells from time to time," Grey teased.

She laughed. "I imagine it's easier on the purse anyway. My late husband was an inveterate gambler, so I understand the appeal of the card tables." As they were each handed a paper, she said, "You will find the various games in each of these rooms."

As she moved to speak with some other guests, Sebastian folded the paper and tucked it neatly into his pocket. "I shouldn't be needing this. My interest will be piqued wherever I can find a certain lady." After a scandalous wink at Grey, he sauntered off.

Grey, in turn, studied the sheet before him and tried to imagine which entertainment Araminta might enjoy. As he was considering it, he walked past the front parlor where several people were inside, enjoying chess and backgammon, among several others. But it was the two women he spied seated on the floor that captured his attention.

Araminta was a vision in her ivory gown with bits of gold threading, but it was the brilliant smile on her face that temporarily struck him immobile.

Almost without conscious thought he eventually found himself moving forward. "Is there room for one more?" He didn't even know what they were playing, but when Araminta glanced up in surprise and those mesmerizing silver eyes met his gaze, he didn't really care.

"I suppose that would be all right." He thought he saw her breathing catch as she looked across at the rather solemn blond girl. "Do you mind, sweeting?"

The girl shook her head. "No. It's fine."

Grey could tell that the youngest Bevelstroke sister would have preferred that he went away, so as he sat down and joined them, he decided that his first order of business was to put her at ease. With his focus on her, he asked gently, "What are we playing?"

She flicked her gaze toward him and then dropped it back to the floor. "Spillkins," she replied.

"Hmm." He had played the game many times with his sister in the nursery as they were growing up, but this girl didn't know that. "I'm afraid I'm not familiar with the rules."

As he'd hoped, she scooped up the sticks off the floor, adding her own and Araminta's to the pile, and then she let go of them, allowing them to fall into another messy disarray. "The object is to remove the most sticks," Olivia explained. "Without moving the others." She carefully demonstrated, slowly plucking one from the set. "As long as you don't move a stick, then you get another turn. If you do, it passes to the next player. The game is over when the last stick is removed."

"Sounds rather simple," he murmured.

She glanced up at him with a shrug. "It is. You can go first."

Grey gently grabbed hold of one of the sticks and pulled it slowly, but at the last second he yanked a bit too firmly, causing several of the other sticks piled on top to jar loose. He gave a mock wince as he finally turned his head and met Araminta's gaze. "It seems I need more practice."

He was surprised to see the glimmer of moisture in her lovely eyes and wondered at the cause for it. "I believe it's your turn, Lady Araminta," he said softly.

She nodded, but it was obvious she didn't trust herself to speak as she withdrew her own stick from the pile.

He mulled this over as the play continued, until the floor was clear. It was obvious that Olivia was the champion, for she visibly had more sticks. "You were a worthy opponent, Lady Olivia," he said with a hand placed over his heart.

She smiled and said, "I suspect that once you properly learn the game, you will best me quite effortlessly." She got to her feet, and Araminta and Grey followed suit. "If you'll excuse me, I wish to see what refreshments they are offering. Do you want anything, Minty?"

"No, thank you, dearest," Araminta returned. Once her sister was gone, she turned to Grey and said sincerely, "Thank you for being patient with her."

He thought that was rather odd of her to say, so he replied, "Of course. She's a delightful girl. Why would I not?"

She glanced toward her sister and said, "Livy has a certain aversion to public gatherings. She's been like that since she was a child. In such it has made her dreadfully shy and withdrawn, but you caused her to talk to you in such a way that she felt comfortable enough to get some punch without me at her side." She offered him a watery smile. "It meant a lot to me that you were so kind."

"I would be happy to assist any time," he offered sincerely. "Perhaps we could go for a ride in my landau tomorrow, weather permitting."

She smiled slowly. "I'd like that, my lord."

As someone came over to chat with her, Grey couldn't help but stand a little bit taller at her acceptance.

Araminta left the party that evening, her heart warmed in more ways than one. After Olivia had gained some courage, thanks to the attentions of Lord Somers, she had actually started to come out of her shell and begun to flirt with a couple of gentlemen who wished to pay their addresses to her. If Olivia continued to encourage such attention, Araminta was certain that her youngest sister would have a proposal by the New Year, if not sooner, which would make her very happy indeed.

Once they returned home and Livy and Calliope headed upstairs, she held Isadora back to speak with her. When she mentioned the change in Olivia, and the ensuing ride with the earl the following day, Isa nodded in approval. "I agree that this would be the best thing for our Livy. I think she would be quite happy properly settled and wed with a family of her own." Her grey eyes narrowed slightly. "What I want to know is, what exactly is your relationship with Lord Somers? He's beginning to appear quite a bit in our lives lately."

Araminta gave a slight laugh, although her eyes shifted away from her sister. "There is nothing between us, of course."

"I don't think that's true."

She sighed. "If we have the chance to encourage Olivia to break out of herself, would you have me deny it? She responds to Lord Somers, Isa. Should I deny him her company?"

"And what if he should be the one to make her an offer?" Isa countered softly. "What then?"

Araminta crossed her arms and shrugged. "Naturally, I would be happy for them." *Liar,* her conscience accused, but she shoved it aside.

"I suppose if that's what you wish to tell yourself." Isadora paused. "I just don't want to see you get hurt." With that, she quit the room.

After she was gone, Araminta sank down onto the settee. She hadn't allowed herself to think about Lord Somers in any other way than a hopeful suitor who was doomed for disappointment, and yet, after the considerate way he'd been with Olivia that evening, she definitely saw him in a different light. Not only was he handsome and charming company, but he was also proving that he wasn't the unrepentant rake that she'd originally thought. Unlike his companion, Lord Blakely, the earl had a care for others beyond himself.

And yet, that didn't mean she shouldn't be cautious around him. He could easily be a man that she could find herself drawn to, and for a woman who wished to live without the strictures of a husband; it would be detrimental to her ultimate goal in making her own way.

She squared her shoulders and stood. She needed her rest and sitting there and allowing her mind to run wild would accomplish nothing. As she entered her room, her maid assisted her out of her gown and stays and then took her leave while Araminta changed into her nightdress.

However, it was after she was tucked into her bed that the true disturbing visions of Lord Somers refused to abate. She dreamt of what it might be like to kiss him, to have those glorious hands caress her skin. She tossed and turned most of the night while her heart raced inside of her chest and her body burned with desire.

When the dawn finally arrived, she was exhausted, but more than that, she feared that Isadora might be correct.

If she wasn't careful, she could give Lord Somers the power to break her heart.

And that wasn't acceptable.

CHAPTER 4

Grey had been rather excited about seeing Araminta again. He thought they'd had a moment last evening, and he was hoping that meant he was starting to win the lady over. But he would have to tread carefully. He didn't want her to imagine that he was only being nice to Lady Olivia to be in Araminta's good graces. If the youngest Bevelstroke sister suffered from public gatherings, he wanted to be able to do what he could to set her at ease. She was certainly lovely enough that, if introduced to the right gentleman, she would start to blossom like the undiscovered rose she was.

Araminta, on the other hand, had fully bloomed. It was this strong, self-reliant woman who had instantly captured his interest to the point he feared he would easily do anything she asked, if only she would agree to be his.

He strode up the steps to the door of their house the next afternoon, and handed his card over to the butler who answered. He removed his top hat as he waited in the foyer, but wasn't forced to cool his heels for long as the object of his fascination walked down the stairs with her younger sister in tow.

He could barely tear his eyes away from Araminta. She was a

vision dressed in a white gown with a dark orange velvet pelisse and matching bonnet over that becoming chestnut hair. She carried a brown fur muff in her grasp. He didn't know many women who could wear such an unusual shade without some sort of impediment, but it only highlighted the color on her face and the shade of her brilliant eyes as she greeted him. "Good day, Lord Somers."

His enthusiasm dimmed somewhat, for he thought he might have earned a bit more regard, but while she was cordial, her greeting was void of any sort of the anticipation he felt flowing through his veins. Nevertheless, he was as cordial as ever. "Lady Araminta." He offered a light bow and then turned to the girl at her side. "And Lady Olivia. I'm pleased that you both accepted my invitation."

"I'm glad you sent 'round a note so we would know what to expect," Araminta returned evenly. "Although I daresay I was surprised you mentioned ice skating. It's been an age since I went."

He bestowed his most appealing grin, the one that normally had women swooning at his feet. "Then, as I see it, it's high past time you indulged the sport. I, for one, shall be the toast of London with two beautiful ladies at my side." He grinned. "Perhaps I should have invited your other two sisters along as well so that I would be even more envied."

Olivia giggled, although her sister remained visibly unaffected. Grey withheld a frown, as he definitely decided that he would have to increase his level of courtship. He thought about flowers and various gifts to show his interest, but something told him that wouldn't impress Araminta. She was entirely too set on her path to allow a bouquet of lilies to sway her mind. For her to think of him in a romantic light, he would have to perform some sort of heroic act.

"There's no need to worry on that score, my lord," Olivia said merrily. "Calliope is out this afternoon, and Isa prefers to walk instead of glide along the ice."

He'd instructed that the top of the landau remain down for their outing, although he'd made sure to provide for the comfort of his guests with a warming brick.

As he gestured to his driver that they were ready to depart, he donned his hat once more and then settled across from the sisters. "How are you enjoying London thus far, Lady Olivia?"

She was dressed in a striking royal blue ensemble and as her blond head turned to him, he saw that her cheeks were already turning a becoming shade of rose from the cold. It was either that, or she was embarrassed at being put on the spot. Either way, Grey thought it was endearing and put him in mind of his own sister when they were younger and embarked on adventures together. When he glanced at Araminta to gauge her reaction, she was regarding him with a considering expression, likely trying to make out his true character. He was determined that she discover he wasn't at all like Lord Blakely. At least… not any longer.

Not since he'd met *her*.

"I'm not exactly sure what to think yet, my lord," Olivia replied in a delicate voice. "It's quite different from the country."

"Indeed, it is. But there are several shops that might be of interest to you. Surely you've taken a stroll down Bond Street by now?"

"I have," she admitted. "But I don't really care about the latest fashions like my sister, Calliope."

He thought for a moment and gathering what he knew about her, he made another suggestion. "In that case you might find Hatchard's on Piccadilly more to your liking. They have a vast array of books if you like to read. And, of course, Gunter's Tea Shop in Berkeley Square is incomparable. If you go, make sure and try the burnt filbert cream ice. It's my favorite."

Her face broke out into a wreath of smiles. "Thank you for the suggestion, Lord Somers. I certainly shall."

~

Araminta couldn't decide whether to remain on her guard around the earl—or fly across the carriage and smother him in relentless kisses. Her face warmed at the very idea, and if he noticed she hoped he would believe it was from the chill in the air. Either way, the broad smile on her sister's face, the first true one she'd revealed since they had arrived in London, made all of Araminta's uncertainty worthwhile.

As they rode into the park, Araminta noticed that the crowd was no smaller than the one from the day before. If anything, the snow had brought more people out. She saw children tossing snowballs at one another, while some even rolled about in the fluff, much to the dismay of their nearby governesses.

"We haven't had much snow in the past two years," Lord Somers noted, as if reading her mind. "So when it does appear, it's quite a treat. Perhaps after we skate, we might build a snowman."

Olivia gasped at the prospect and Araminta's heart melted even more toward their escort.

They stopped near the bank of the Thames where vendors were selling everything from roasted chestnuts to hot chocolate, and of course, there was someone who was renting metal blade skates. Araminta had brought their own blades and once they alighted from the carriage and trudged through the snow along the edge of the river, they each strapped their own pair to the bottoms of their boots.

"Did you know that the first skates were made of bone?" the earl noted.

"Were they?" Olivia asked curiously.

"Indeed. And while what you see before you may be impressive, London has actually held Frost Fairs on the surface of the ice, the Thames would freeze so solidly. The last one was in 1814 and nearly a dozen printing presses were out there, readily printing up a commemorative poem in honor of the event."

"How fascinating!" Olivia breathed. "Do you think they will have another?"

He shrugged. "I couldn't say. After that time we've had rather mild winters and with the talk of demolishing the old bridge I fear the water will flow too heavily to enjoy much longer."

"Then we shouldn't waste one more moment!" Olivia took off across the icy exterior with a joyous laugh.

Araminta couldn't help but join in the merriment. But when she glanced at the earl, the intensity of his blue eyes froze her laughter.

As she sobered, he turned his focus back to where Olivia was gliding along. "She looks free."

Araminta hugged herself. "She does." She snorted. "It's rather ironic because she detests the cold, but when it comes to ice skating, she is perfectly content. It's as if she doesn't even feel it."

They stood there side by side for a moment and then a hand appeared in her line of vision. Araminta admired the fine stitching of the material and yet found herself wondering if the flesh beneath would be as soft. Tamping down her curiosity, she turned to gaze at the earl, captured by the rather appealing smile that tilted up only one corner of his mouth. "Shall we?"

Araminta's heart pounded in her chest, but she slowly slipped her gloved hand in his. Strong fingers wrapped around hers, and with a gentle pull, he guided her onto the frozen ice.

At first, her legs protested the slick surface, but it didn't take her long to gain her balance, having enjoyed this same activity many times as a child. But even after she no longer felt as though she might tumble onto her arse, he kept hold of her hand, and she decided that she didn't really mind. In truth, it was rather... nice.

She glanced at her companion and found that he didn't have any issue standing upright. He looked as confident about skating as he did about anything else he did. Dressed in a navy blue waistcoat and buff trousers and a black greatcoat flying out behind him, he was quite dashing. She also couldn't help but note that she wasn't the only one who thought so. As they moved along, several envious glances from other female skaters were shot their way. Araminta merely lifted her chin a bit higher and smiled as if she was having a grand time, when in truth, she was.

"You're a rather accomplished skater," she said.

He glanced at her with a smile that was almost rakish in nature. "I've had plenty of practice. You weren't the only one who spent most of the time in the country. My sister and I used to head to our pond quite often either to skate in the winter, or fish in the summer."

She tilted her head slightly. "Somehow I can't envision you sitting along a grassy bank with a pole in your grasp."

He held her gaze. "You'll find that there is much to learn about me if you would allow yourself to do so."

Araminta's breath caught at the blatant invitation in those eyes. She looked away and stared at the ice beneath her, hoping that she could gather her thoughts before they completely scattered to the wind.

"Have you ever spun on the ice?"

She was relieved that he turned the subject back to something more neutral. "I—" She hesitated. "I don't think I ever tried."

With a wide grin, he said nothing more, just pulled her around so that they were face to face. He grasped her other hand and said, "We shall dance on the ice. Just follow my lead."

As he began to skate forward, she did the same in the opposite direction. Once they had built up speed, he turned his skates outward and with their momentum pulling them around, Araminta did the same. Spinning about like a top, she laughed at the sheer joy of it all. She hadn't been this carefree in some time. While her father had never been so strict as to inhibit their outdoor play, she admitted that her determination to do things on her own terms had swallowed up any sort of personal freedoms that she might have otherwise had.

When they finally slowed to a stop, she fell forward and he caught her easily, their arms encircling each other. With the blood still pumping steadily through her veins, she glanced up into his face. It was inches away. "I'm dizzy," she remarked breathlessly.

His focus moved over her face, coming to rest on her mouth. "It happens," he murmured. "Some of the best things in life can make one rather dazed."

Araminta abruptly stilled, her smile fading away, for something told her that he wasn't speaking of skating any longer.

Grey wondered what she would do if he gave in to the impulse to kiss her. The urge was so strong that he was filled with the anticipation, the moment that his mouth would press against hers. She looked so lovely in that moment that he would be hard pressed to think of anything else. Her silver eyes were sparkling with the brilliance of the Christmas star. Her full, rosy lips were parted slightly; the dark curls peeking out from beneath her bonnet framing her face rather adoringly.

In that moment, he knew that there would be no other woman for him. He wasn't sure how she'd managed it, but Lady Araminta Bevelstroke had quite bewitched him.

And she didn't even know the power she held over him.

He started to lower his head, and it was as if time stood still.

"She fell through the ice!"

Grey stopped and turned to where the warning had been shouted. There was frantic pointing as a pair of flailing arms in blue struggled to return to the surface along a deserted section farther downriver.

His heart stuttered in his chest, for that attire looked vaguely familiar, but it was Araminta's gasp of horror that proved his suspicions.

"Oh, my God." She covered her mouth with her hand and instantly paled. "It's Olivia!" She started to rush forward, and Grey was right on her heels.

A crowd had started to gather around the area where the woman was crying out for help. "I'm coming, Livy!" Araminta shouted as she began to push her way through the people, scared to draw any closer, for fear that the ice wouldn't hold.

It wasn't until Araminta was close to Olivia that Grey heard the dreaded pop of the ice starting to break even further.

He grabbed her arm and kept her immobile. She flashed him an angry glare. "Let go of me! My sister—!"

"It won't hold both of you!" he snapped. "And I don't need to rescue two Bevelstroke women today." He threw a hand out to the people gathered around. "Get out of here! Get off the ice!"

The onlookers scattered as Araminta glanced down at the ice, as if finally noticing the cracks beneath her feet. Grey unstrapped his skates and tossed them aside, along with his hat, and then he dropped to his stomach, thinking that approaching Olivia by this angle might be the best way to get her out of the freezing water without causing more stress on the cracking ice before they both went under. Either way, there was no time to waste, for already he could see that her lips were starting to turn blue.

He began to crawl toward her. "It's going to be all right, Lady Olivia." She nodded her head, her teeth chattering as she clung desperately to the edge of the ice, so she wouldn't be lost to the current beneath.

If that happened…

Grey wasn't even going to finish that thought.

He was almost close enough to reach out his hand to her when there was another loud pop beneath him. He stilled for a moment, waiting to see if it would hold, and when nothing happened, he moved forward and reached out a hand to her. "Grab my hand! We have to hurry!"

She strained as she reached out to him, and as her fingers met his, he grabbed hold of her. "Swim toward me," he instructed.

He could tell her strength was starting to wane, the cold making her immobile, but she was strong like her sister and with a combined effort, she finally lifted her torso up out of the water. Grey released the breath he'd been holding, but they weren't free of danger just yet. He began to slide backward and pull her along with him as he went.

He thought that they might actually survive this, but just as her legs became free, the ominous sound of more cracking met his ears. "Dear God," he breathed, as the ice began to give way beneath Olivia once more.

"Crawl to me, Olivia! *Now!*"

Fear shone in her green eyes, and he was starting to worry that she would be lost if they didn't get away soon. She tried her best to struggle to her hands and knees, but she kept falling back to the ice, her sodden skirts impeding her progress. Sweat broke out on his forehead as he struggled to pull her and get her away from the perilous situation they found themselves in.

It came as a surprise when another masculine arm joined his. He didn't even look to see who it was, merely thankful for the extra assistance.

Together the two men managed to pull Olivia to the safety of the nearest bank. Her bonnet was missing and her blond hair was lying about her shoulders in a tangled mess, but all of it was inconsequential. The main focus was getting her warm before a dangerous chill set in.

Grey glanced at Araminta who was standing to the side, tears shining in her eyes. He could tell she wanted to comfort her sister, and when the stranger lifted Olivia into his arms and began to walk toward a black lacquered coach, Grey grabbed hold of Araminta's arm and said, "Go with them. I'll follow in my carriage."

She blinked, as if coming out of a daze and began to rush toward the retreating figure carrying Olivia.

Grey noted the crest on the coach and thought it odd that Miles Stone, the Duke of Gravesend, would be out at such a public gathering like this. He was known as the "Elusive Duke" because he was seldom seen among society following the injuries he'd sustained at Waterloo, which, if rumor was to be believed, were quite extensive. While he saw no outward impediment to the man, he knew quite well that not all injuries were visible.

Grey rushed toward the landau and ordered his driver to take him to Grosvenor Square posthaste.

CHAPTER 5

Just before the door of the coach shut in her face, Araminta stopped it with her palm. "I don't know who you are, sir, but you aren't going anywhere with my sister without *me*."

The piercing obsidian eyes glared at her through the gloom. His dark hair was longer than was fashionable and tied back in a queue that was several years out of date, although his greatcoat and Hessians proclaimed that he was a gentleman. "Get in," he rasped.

Araminta didn't hesitate as she climbed inside, although she wondered what this man was about taking off with Olivia like he had. As he rapped on the roof of the velvet-lined coach, complete with carriage lanterns and all the amenities one might find among the wealthy, she demanded, "Does your driver know where you're going? You didn't even ask where we lived."

"That's because I don't care," he returned in that same husky murmur. "I'm taking her to see a personal, trusted physician."

She crossed her arms and frowned. "That's very presumptuous of you. Don't you think that should be my choice to make?"

He eyed her steadily, his dark eyes boring straight through

her soul. "You haven't been in London long. Surely you wish to see her treated by a professional doctor rather than some surgical quack if you want her to live."

Araminta couldn't believe the audacity of this man. She'd believed him to be a savior, but he was turning out to be anything but a hero. "Who are you?"

He paused, as if he didn't wish to answer, but then he said, "The Duke of Gravesend."

"My father was a duke as well," she pointed out. "But I can assure you that he was never quite so crass as to abduct someone's sister, no matter the reason."

He lowered his head, as if suddenly contrite, but then she realized that he was merely looking upon Olivia's face. Her sister was still shivering uncontrollably, but her eyes were closed. It was difficult to tell if she was asleep or just doing her best to forget the harrowing incident. "She reminds me of someone I used to know, someone I couldn't save," he said softly.

This admission took Araminta aback. She wanted to know more, but decided she would let the rumor mill offer up those missing pieces, as it wasn't her place to pry, nor was it the time.

The coach came to a halt and he said curtly, "We're here."

Without waiting for a footman to open the door, he climbed out with Olivia still clutched in his arms and strode up to the door of a building that proclaimed it belonged to Dr. Thierry Haimlin. Araminta was right behind him.

He pounded on the door with his foot and stood impatiently while he waited for his summons to be answered. Moments later a light-haired gentleman with glasses and who Araminta would guess was in his mid-thirties, stood in the frame dressed in buff trousers, a white cambric shirt, and a brown and gold waistcoat. "Your Grace—" Araminta wasn't sure if he was more surprised to see the duke on his doorstep, or the fact he was holding an unconscious woman. Either way, he recovered quickly as he ushered them inside.

He led them to a simply furnished parlor where the duke laid Olivia gently down on the settee. "What happened?" The doctor inquired as he retrieved a black medical bag and began to examine her.

"She fell through the ice," the duke returned somberly.

"How long was she in the water?"

"About ten minutes I would say."

Dr. Haimlin lifted his head and said, "Her heart rate sounds normal, so that is a good sign, but we need to get her out of these wet clothes and get some warm broth into her. She will also need to be monitored for the next twenty-four hours to ensure that fever doesn't set in. I can set her up in one of my patient rooms upstairs if that is amenable." He looked to Araminta. "I assume she is of some relation to you?"

"Yes." She nodded. "She's my sister, Lady Olivia Bevelstroke, and I support whatever you think will ensure her full recovery."

"Very good. If you would follow me?"

The duke carried Olivia upstairs and they entered a sparse room with nothing more than a fireplace, a bed, and a washstand. Gravesend stepped out of the room while the doctor sent in a maid to assist Araminta in undressing her sister. Once she was stripped completely bare, a simple white nightdress was put over her head and she was tucked underneath a warm coverlet. Another maid brought up a tray with tea and broth and Araminta did what she could to coerce Olivia to eat. Although she was still rather incoherent, she managed to get a few sips down, and Araminta was thankful to see that some of her natural color had returned to her cheeks. She didn't want to see any more of that dreadfully pale, bluish tinge ever again.

Once Olivia had fallen into an easy slumber, Araminta left the room and went downstairs. The duke was standing by the mantel, but he turned at her entrance. "How is she?"

"Resting comfortably," she offered.

He visibly relaxed at her reassurance. "I'm glad to hear it."

"While I don't wish to leave my sister, I fear that my other sisters will be concerned if I don't return home and tell them what has happened. They have no idea where I am."

He bowed lightly. "Allow me to offer you the use of my coach."

As they headed to Grosvenor Square, Araminta leaned her head back against the velvet seat. The fear that had struck her earlier had melted into a terrible exhaustion.

"I hope you aren't upset that I took your sister to see Dr. Haimlin, instead of taking her home." She glanced over at the duke who was looking down at his lap. "I just knew she needed immediate care and he was someone I could trust implicitly."

"I was rather irritated at first," Araminta acknowledged. "But you were right. It would have taken much longer for him to arrive at the house, and I daresay I wouldn't have chosen anyone but Dr. Haimlin to treat her. He seems to be a very kind man."

"He is the best," the duke said adamantly.

When they arrived at the townhouse, she said, "Would you like to come in for some tea?" She knew it sounded rather inane, but she was at a loss of what to say.

"Thank you, but no." He smiled tightly. "I should be getting home. My mother will no doubt insist that I help her with the Christmas Eve ball she has planned in a fortnight."

Araminta's memory sparked and she realized why the duke's name suddenly seemed familiar to her. "Yes, we've accepted the duchess' invitation."

"Indeed." He returned almost thoughtfully. "Then I may decide to join the party after all."

With that parting remark, Araminta stepped down from the carriage as the duke drove away. Never before had she met such an enigma. But she intended to ensure that society knew of his kindness to her family.

Araminta noticed that Lord Somers' carriage was still parked outside, and the moment she stepped in the door, her sisters came rushing out into the foyer to greet her. She also noticed the earl, although he hung back, remaining in the doorway of the parlor.

"The earl told us what happened! How frightening!" Calliope's eyes were filled with tears as she embraced her.

"How is Olivia? For that matter, *where* is she?" Isa asked.

Araminta explained the turn of events. Calliope's eyes widened with each word she uttered.

When she'd finished, Isadora said, "I think you've done enough for today, Minty. You should get some rest. I'll go tend Olivia."

"I'm coming with you," Calliope said firmly.

Araminta couldn't help but smile. If nothing else could be said of her dear sisters, it was that they were all there for one another.

As Isadora began to speak to the butler about readying the carriage, Lord Somers stepped forward. "Use my landau. I'll instruct my driver to take you anywhere you wish to go. It will be quicker and I can take a hackney home."

"Thank you, Lord Somers," Isadora said as she set her bonnet on her head and buttoned her pelisse. "Your generosity will not be forgotten." She pointedly glanced at Araminta, and then with Calliope at her side, they walked out the front door.

"YOU LOOK like you could use some tea," Grey said once they were alone. "Or perhaps something a bit stronger."

He could see the lines of strain about the lady's mouth, but his statement made her smile, erasing some of the tension that had been present. "Indeed. I think a bit of sherry should do the trick."

When she followed him into the parlor, he pointed to the settee. "Sit. I'll pour."

He walked over to the sideboard and Araminta didn't argue as she sank down onto the plush seat. "It doesn't seem right that I'm the hostess and yet, you're serving me."

Grey returned and handed her the drink. He pressed the crystal tumbler into her hand and murmured, "You've been through a rather trying ordeal."

She snorted. "I certainly didn't picture today going as it has."

He sat down next to her, careful to keep his distance, and crossed one leg over the other. "Indeed. But then, life generally doesn't operate the way we believe it should."

She took a fortifying sip of her sherry and then lowered the glass to her lap. "No, it certainly doesn't."

They fell silent for a time, the only sound in the room coming from the crackling fire in the hearth. But Grey liked it. He realized that he could enjoy a companionable quiet with Araminta without it being awkward. It was merely another notch in her favor when it came to being his perfect match.

"Thank you, Lord Somers."

He looked into those lovely silver eyes. "For what? I believe it was the duke that saved the day."

"No." She shook her head. "It was all you. If you hadn't acted when you did, things wouldn't have progressed as quickly as they had." She reached out and took his hand, giving it a light squeeze. "You are the one who saved my sister's life."

Grey swallowed heavily. He wasn't used to such praise. It made him uncomfortable. That was why he'd been a rake for so many years. "I was just doing what needed to be done."

She smiled. "I think you're being modest."

"And I think you're beautiful."

Grey hadn't meant to say the words out loud. They just slipped out of his mouth around the foot he'd obviously shoved in there. But there was no use retracting them, nor denying the claim when it was nothing short of the truth.

"Lord Somers..."

Her tone was hesitant and he cursed himself for being too forward. "Forgive me. I... er, should be going."

Grey started to rise to his feet, but a gentle hand on his arm made him pause. He turned back to Araminta, and now he saw the yearning in her eyes. "I'm not upset with you for the compliment," she assured him. "I was just going to say that—" She looked uncertain for a moment and then settled with, "I enjoy your company."

Grey would have given his right arm to know what she'd actually been going to say, but the fact that she'd admitted she enjoyed being around him was another point in his favor. But since he didn't want to play all of his cards too early, he asked, "What do you like to do for fun? Other than Spillkins, of course."

She laughed and he was quite sure he'd never heard anything quite so appealing. "I think I have a deck of cards around here if you're up for a whist challenge." She lifted a dark brow at him and he nearly growled with the hunt.

"You may regret your choice of entertainment, for I've been known to lighten many purses with my skill."

Her lips twitched. "Perhaps. But that was before you met me."

BY THE TIME Isadora and Calliope returned it was dusk. Until then, Araminta hadn't realized how late it had gotten. She'd been so wrapped up with the earl that time had quite ceased to exist. She couldn't recall having so much fun playing cards since her father had passed. Her sisters certainly didn't care for whist as much as she did.

She could tell by Isa's direct expression that she was wondering just how close they were becoming. Calliope headed straight for the leftover biscuits on the tea tray and popped one into her mouth as she took a seat on the settee. She didn't even try to hide her curiosity as she studied them.

Araminta adopted an even tone. "How is Olivia?"

"Very well," Isa returned. "She was awake when we arrived and even talked to us for quite a while. I imagine once she is cleared of any fever, the doctor will release her to come home tomorrow."

Araminta put a hand to her heart in genuine relief. "Thank goodness."

"Indeed," Lord Somers noted. He glanced out the window. "On that note, I should be going."

Isadora tilted her head to the side. "Don't leave on our account."

He bowed slightly. "I would never do you the dishonor. I fear it's later than I expected and it's been a rather trying day for us all. And I daresay if I play one more hand of whist with your sister I'm going to wonder at my own abilities. As it is, my ego is rather deflated."

Calliope laughed and interjected, "That was your first mistake. No one ever beats Araminta at whist. Our father was proficient at the game and taught her every single trick."

With that, he turned his blue gaze back on the object of his desire. "And here I thought we were friends, Lady Araminta. It appears I shall have to be more cautious in the future when it comes to any sort of recreational activity. Who knows? You might intentionally trod upon my toes at a ball."

Araminta clasped her hands before her. "Only if you deserved it."

Her breath caught when he winked at her right before he walked out the door.

However, the slight warmth she was feeling quickly changed when Isadora walked over to sit in the spot the earl had just vacated. "What's going on, Minty?"

"Nothing." She shrugged. Although, rather than meeting her sister's knowing gaze, she began to carefully gather up the cards that were still strewn about the table.

"I think she *likes* him," Calliope piped up in a singsong voice.

Araminta rolled her eyes, but she decided the safest approach to this discussion was to give a portion of the truth. The rest, she didn't yet care to divulge to herself. "Lord Somers is very amenable. After what he did for Olivia today, I daresay I owe him a debt of gratitude."

"It didn't look like mere *gratitude* I was witnessing when I walked in," Isadora pointed out.

"That's because you only look at things how you want to see them," Araminta snapped, losing the thread on her patience as she stood. "Rest assured there is nothing between the earl and I other than a polite acquaintance. I fully intend to live life on my own terms. Now, if you'll excuse me, it's been a long afternoon and I wish to retire."

Araminta didn't wait for her elder sister to reply and ignored the smug expression Calliope wore as she munched on another biscuit.

As she reached the sanctity of her bedchamber, she shut the door and closed her eyes. It was only in private that she allowed herself to think of the earl. Here she could fantasize about him without any inhibitions. There had been a moment before they had begun their card game when she thought he was about to kiss her and she wondered what she would have done if he had. She bit her lip, for something told her that she wouldn't have pushed him away, but drawn him closer.

She put a hand to her forehead as she began to pace about the room. She couldn't be falling for the earl! It must be the romantic aspect of the Christmas season that was getting under her skin, rather than any true feelings of love tugging at her heartstrings. To believe otherwise would ruin everything that she'd planned for herself. She would lose her freedom, her very *identity* as a woman if she married, for that would allow her husband to take control of not just her finances, but her livelihood.

Araminta shook her head. While she was becoming rather fond of Lord Somers, she would draw the line at anything going further between them.

She snorted ironically, for she'd told herself that very thing just this morning, but following Olivia's accident, she hadn't been worried about safeguarding her emotions, concern for her sister's welfare at the forefront of her mind.

Henceforth, she wouldn't make any further errors in judgment.

CHAPTER 6

The next morning a note was sent over from Dr. Haimlin with the good news that Olivia could be released from his care. Araminta, along with Isadora and Calliope, headed over to the clinic to gather their youngest sibling. When they walked into her room, they were overjoyed to see that she was sitting up and looked perfectly healthy.

"Oh, Livy!" Tears stung Araminta's eyes as the harrowing incident from the day before struck her, and she realized how different things could be right now.

"Don't cry, Minty," that sweet voice replied. She reached out a hand and Araminta grasped it with both of hers. The warmth that radiated from her sister's palm made her eyes flood with even more moisture.

"I can't help it, dearest. I was so afraid when I realized that you had fallen through the ice."

Olivia smiled gently. "I'm just sorry I lost my skates."

Araminta laughed. "I will buy you ten pair for Christmas!"

"Ooh! Look at all the flowers!"

Araminta glanced at Calliope, who was standing by a large bouquet of white lilies. She withdrew the card and read,

"Wishing you a quick recovery. Signed the Earl of Somers." A red brow lifted smugly at Araminta as she replaced the note and moved to the bouquet of yellow roses and plucked out the next card. "Hmm. There's nothing written, but it's signed Gravesend."

"The duke," Isadora murmured, and exchanged a glance with Araminta. She knew what her sister was thinking, that he would be a lovely prospect for Olivia.

"I don't really recall him," Olivia said quietly.

Isadora moved forward. "Perhaps you'll have a chance to reacquaint yourself with each other sooner than you think. His mother is in charge of the Christmas Eve ball." She smiled gently. "That is, if you're feeling up to it by then. I shouldn't wish to rush your recovery and cause a setback."

Olivia nodded, but said nothing more on the matter.

Isadora brought forth the dress they had procured from her wardrobe, and together they helped Olivia into the mauve gown. Calliope moved forward and threaded her arm through hers. "Let's get you home. I daresay I'm eager to catch you up on the latest London gossip."

She led Olivia out of the room while Isadora and Araminta gathered the flowers and followed them to their waiting carriage.

When they arrived at the townhouse, Araminta noticed a familiar figure sitting atop his horse. She glanced to Isadora as she handed over her bouquet to a waiting footman. "I'll be just a moment."

Isadora said nothing, but the slightly condemning look on her face spoke volumes as she disappeared inside the house with her sisters. "Good day, Lord Somers." Araminta greeted him cordially.

He tipped his hat at her. "Lady Araminta. I see Olivia has made it home safely. Dare I hope that means she suffers no ill effects from her dip in the freezing Thames?"

"She's doing very well." She paused, unsure of what to say in the bright light of a new day. She twisted her hands before her. "The flowers you sent were beautiful."

He smiled broadly. "I can only hope they lifted her spirits." He hesitated and then added, "And yours."

Araminta's heart sank. The earl was being so considerate that she didn't want him to believe that she was being overtly discourteous if she told him that their association could never be more than what it was, but Isadora's taunting reminder the day before kept replaying over in her mind. She had been the one who had insisted they could make their own way in society without the bonds of matrimony. To go back on her word nearly the moment they set foot in London would make her appear the worst sort of hypocrite in all of her sibling's eyes. If she didn't wish to break their trust in her, she had to let the earl go.

"Is something amiss, Lady Araminta?"

She clasped her hands before her and did her best to appear unaffected by what she was about to do. "Actually, my lord, there is. After yesterday, I realized that I've been selfish in allowing my fondness for you to overrule my good sense. I have enjoyed our interludes more than you can imagine, but I fear this must go no further than a polite acquaintance. My sisters come first, as they always have. We have made a vow to stick together, and I intend to honor that promise."

GREY'S HEART was pounding as if he'd run a considerable distance, although he hadn't moved an inch. "I see." Perhaps he'd been coming on too strong. After all, he wasn't used to courting a lady to ensure that it went beyond a temporary affair. "Perhaps if I gave you some time—"

"No. I'm afraid that it's just not possible." She offered him a tight smile, and he had to wonder if it was because she was growing irritated with him and trying not to let her frustration show, or if it was something... more. "I must go. Good day, my lord."

She was gone before he could even call out her name. But as she disappeared inside the house, he glanced at the parlor window as the curtain fell back into place, but not before he saw a dark head move away. He frowned lightly, but he supposed that answered his earlier thought. He would bet his horse that Lady Isadora was behind Araminta's reticence to retain his company.

He urged his mount forward and wondered if he shouldn't just reconsider his choice and find someone else to wed, but at the same time he realized it would be a fruitless endeavor. While females on the hunt for a title were plentiful in London, he wanted someone who saw him as Greyson Hartfield and not just the Earl of Somers.

But how would he go about charming that dragon of a sister?

He abruptly smiled, for he realized that *he* wouldn't need to. There was someone he had in mind that would be perfect for the job.

Grey made a detour and headed for White's, where he knew the gentleman he was looking for would likely be. He'd met Remington Fletcher, the Marquess of Osgood, through a combined business venture to see the first steam locomotive railroad come to pass in England. An eight-mile stretch of track from Stockton to Darlington that easily and more efficiently transported coal to the ships on the coast for easier shipment had turned out to be a very profitable investment for both of them. Even though the line had opened just three months prior, the amount that could be hauled was more than double than if carted by wagon and horses alone.

And considering they had embarked on one successful journey together, Grey decided that they could do it again.

He walked through the doors of the hallowed walls of the men's only exclusive club and found Rem right where he knew he'd be, seated at the Duke of Wellington's honored table near the front bow window, whose distinction had included Beau Brummell and Lord Alvanley in the past. To be offered a seat there was likened to being sent an invitation as a personal guest to the palace.

With one leg crossed over the other, a glass of brandy at his elbow and holding a paper in his grasp, Grey knew it was Rem simply because of the russet colored hair that was visible beneath the print. Very few men of his acquaintance had such copper-colored hair, but Rem likely got his in light of his Scottish ancestry. There were rumors that he was a descendant from a distant line of Highland lairds, but as far as Grey knew, he'd never bothered to confirm nor deny the birthright, for he had little to do with those roots, preferring his comfortable life in England.

"You lead such an exciting life, Osgood, considering you spend most of your time here rather than at home. What is so fascinating about London if you never choose to partake of its particular delights?"

A snort preceded the paper as a corner was brought down to reveal the marquess' dry expression. "And what would you have me do, Somers? Attend every ball hoping that I might be mobbed by a marriage-minded mother hoping to foist her empty headed chit at my feet?"

Grey shrugged. "It wouldn't hurt for you to set up a nursery now that you are well off."

The paper was put back in place. "Indeed. I shall consider it the moment you wish to settle down," he muttered, and it was obvious he thought Grey would do no such thing.

"Actually, there *is* someone..."

This time the newsprint was carefully folded and set to the side as the marquess crossed his arms over his chest. "I daresay I never imagined I would live to see the day that the Earl of Somers was brought to heel." He waved a hand toward the empty seat across from him, and Grey sat down. The moment he did, a waiter walked over to take his order. The servant returned shortly thereafter with the same brandy that Osgood had chosen.

Grey took a fortifying sip and relished the soothing, rich flavor as it slid down his throat. With a sigh, he said, "Surely you didn't imagine that my mother would allow me to remain single forever, did you? Besides," he shrugged his shoulders. "This woman is... different."

"I can't imagine how," the marquess drawled. "They all become rather tiring after a time."

Grey focused on the activity outside the window. "Not Lady Araminta."

There was a brief pause before his companion said, "Are you referring to the Duke of Marlington's gels?"

Grey's gaze slid back. "I see word gets around."

"Naturally, but this particular bit of information was provided by Viscount Blakely. He told me about how you were enamored by some chit at the theatre, and then kept rambling on about a red-haired vixen invading his dreams."

Grey shook his head. "I should have known Seb couldn't keep his mouth shut. Although he seemed just as taken with Lady Calliope, the red-haired vixen in question who happens to be Lady Araminta's sister."

"Ah." The marquess nodded. "It's good to know that he hasn't entirely lost his mind. After that conversation, it certainly gave me cause to wonder if he was truly mad."

"Sebastian is many things, but I assure you he is quite sane."

"I daresay I'm intrigued. If you aren't here to discuss Lord Blakely's psyche, then I'm rather curious as to why you've sought me out?" He frowned. "Unless you've heard something about the railroad that has escaped my solicitor?"

"Not at all," Grey assured him. "As far as I know, everything is moving along quite smoothly on the coast." He sat forward slightly and clasped his hands on the table between them. "I would, however, like to ask a particular favor of you."

When the marquess remained silent, Grey pushed forward. "I have been trying to court Lady Araminta, but I've found there is an... impediment keeping me from getting too close."

Rem smiled. "Don't tell me you've lost your charm, Somers?"

Grey allowed the barb to pass. "I had been doing rather well in gaining the lady's favor—until her elder sister interceded. Apparently, all four sisters have made a pledge not to marry and to make their own way as independent women of means. Lady Isadora seems to be making sure that goal is adhered to."

"I see," Rem murmured. "But I fail to see what that has to do with me."

Grey exhaled heavily. "I want you to distract Lady Isadora so I can continue my plans to court her sister."

There was a marked silence after his announcement, and then Osgood threw his head back and laughed richly. He pointed a finger at Grey and spoke in between chuckles. "You nearly had me for a moment, Somers! I appreciate a good lark!"

Grey gritted his teeth. "I wasn't joking."

As the marquess' merriment faded away, his amber eyes widened in mock horror. "You can't be *serious*. Going together on a profitable business venture is one thing, but I see no benefits in this partnership for me."

"Sure there is." Grey grinned broadly. "You will be helping out a close friend."

A copper brow was lifted. "And?"

Grey shoved a hand through his hair. "And I suppose I might be persuaded to sell one of my stallions."

Finally, Osgood's interest was piqued, but then Grey knew the man's one weakness, and it was horseflesh. He spent most of his time at his estate, only venturing to London when it was absolutely necessary. At the moment he was in town because his mother had pleaded with him to escort his niece about in society during her first season. But Grey knew that once Christmas was over, he wouldn't see him again until spring, and that was only if his niece didn't gain a marriage proposal before then.

"I'll consider it."

Grey knew that was all he was going to get at the moment, but still he said, "Don't think on it too long. Christmas is only two weeks away."

With that, he left the marquess to his paper and headed out to find Araminta the perfect gift.

"WHAT IS IT?" Calliope nearly jumped up and down in her excitement surrounding the brown paper wrapped parcel that had been delivered the following morning.

"I can't say." Araminta glanced at her sister as she held the item in question. "Perhaps there's a mix-up and your name should be on it. Are you sure you aren't expecting anything?"

Calliope huffed in exasperation. "It has *your* name on it. Would you just open it?"

Araminta decided that in order to have some peace she would have to do just that. She returned to where she'd been sitting in the parlor working on some embroidery while Isadora was out walking and Olivia was in the library, as usual. Calliope had been working on some correspondence when the butler had brought in the package, which had ensued with the following uproar.

As Araminta peeled back the paper of the mysterious package, she gasped at the image that was revealed.

"What *is* it?" Calliope demanded once more, but when Araminta didn't immediately reply, her sister walked closer to look over her shoulder.

She picked up the painting with the gilt-edged frame. There was a lone woman in the painting, standing before a field with the orange glow of an early morning dawn before her. "It's called 'Woman before the Rising Sun' by Caspar David

Friedrich." She noted a card was carefully tucked behind the frame. She withdrew it and read, "*To celebrate your independence.*"

It wasn't signed, but Araminta didn't have to guess who it was from. She closed her eyes as the haunting vision of Lord Somers flashed behind her lids. She wasn't sure if this painting was meant as a jest since she'd refused any further attentions from him this morning, or even worse, if he had taken her rejection to heart and this was his way of leaving her alone. She sighed, for she wasn't that comfortable with either scenario.

She carefully covered it back up with the paper.

"What are you doing?" Calliope asked.

"Sending it back."

Her sister gasped as she stepped back and then moved around to glare at her. "You can't do that! It's a gift! It would be rude!"

"It's an *improper* one," Araminta said firmly. "A lady mustn't accept gifts from a man unless he is her betrothed or perhaps a devoted suitor. It gives the wrong impression."

"You mean that you might actually like him?" Calliope crossed her arms with a snort. "Because you *do*?"

Araminta stood; the painting tucked under one arm, and faced off with her sister. "Leave it alone, Callie," she snapped. "This has nothing to do with you."

She tried to leave, but her sister was persistent and blocked her path. "It doesn't? And what if I decided that I didn't want to grow into some old spinster like you and Isa? Perhaps I actually *like* the idea of marrying and having a family. Did you ever think of that?"

This caused Araminta to pause. She turned back to Calliope. "Is that what you want?" she asked evenly. "Because when we left the estate we all took a vote and agreed that we wanted to show the world what women of stature could do, other than subject ourselves to the bonds of wedlock."

Calliope shook her head. "Have you ever considered the fact

that marriage doesn't have to be a prison? If you marry for love—"

This time it was Araminta's turn to snort. "That statement just shows how young and naïve you are, Calli. Love fades in time, but marriage vows are forever. What may start out as an equal partnership will eventually turn into something sour."

Calliope barked out a laugh, although her green eyes held censure. "When did you become so jaded in regards to romance? It's not as if you've been thrown over by a recalcitrant beau, or left at the altar. Don't you remember how fondly father spoke of our mothers? *All* of them? I know their regard for him was just as strong, and yet, you would make their unions something sordid and tainted just because you're too scared to risk your heart on anyone!"

For a moment, all Araminta could do was stare at her sister. While Calliope was generally outspoken, this was the first time she'd actually accused her of being some sort of detestable crone. She lifted her chin. "Of course, you're entitled to your opinion, but that doesn't mean it's right." With that, she turned on her heel and left her sister standing in the middle of the parlor to gape at her retreating back.

Although she kept her shoulders rigid and walked away like a mature woman, her eyes stung with emotion. As she shut the door to her bedchamber, she clutched the painting to her chest and leaned against the door with a slow exhale, willing the tears to remain at bay. But her efforts were futile, for a single tear coursed down her cheek.

Dear God, what if Calliope was *right*? What if this endeavor to prove a lady's independence was merely her way of shying away from the heartbreak and disappointment of falling for the *wrong* man? It was true that their father had loved all four of his wives, but there were times she questioned how deeply his devotion had truly gone. Araminta had her reservations that loving *one* person was possible, and yet, the former duke had been enamored of all of their mothers? It just hadn't made sense to her. And she knew she wasn't alone in her thinking. Isadora had said as much on several occasions, which is why they had agreed to leave the estate before the new Duke of Marlington took residence—whoever that might be.

She pressed a hand to her temple and thought back to the day they had made the pact to come to London. Surely they wouldn't have just *told* Calliope and Olivia what they were doing, rather than asking their opinion? But she honestly just couldn't remember.

Frustrated, she knew she would have to speak with Isadora. Not only because of what Calliope had claimed, but also, because she had to know that she wasn't going mad. She moved away from the door and glanced down at the painting in her grasp. She couldn't see the image, for the paper was wrapped around it once more, but knowing that Lord Somers had chosen this gift specifically for her, had *touched* it, warmed her more than she wanted to admit.

Damn Calliope and her foolhardy romantic notions! For now, she was nearly starting to believe in them herself.

CHAPTER 7

Grey had it on good authority, by bribing their downstairs maid, that the Bevelstroke sisters would be attending the reading at the Viscountess Journton's residence that evening. He straightened his cuffs and pulled at his cravat as he entered the drawing room with the Marquess of Osgood, who he was glad to see, had accepted the challenge of at least meeting Lady Isadora Bevelstroke.

"You've straightened your cuffs at least a dozen times since you picked me up," Rem drawled at his side. "I should think much more of your fidgeting would fray the edges."

He huffed a breath. "Can't a man be just a bit nervous at times? Tonight is crucial in my success in wooing Lady Araminta."

The marquess lifted a russet brow. "I thought that depended on me."

"Both, actually," he muttered. He glanced about the assembled, where several chairs had been set up in a semi-circle around a settee taking precedence in the center of the room. "They aren't here yet." He finally took a seat toward the back, close to the entrance.

"Imagine that," the marquess noted. "I doubt anyone is clamoring to join tonight's exciting festivities."

Grey glared at him. "Do you hate Christmas so much?"

"No. I merely dislike sitting for long periods of time without a brandy."

Grey rolled his eyes, but settled in to wait for Araminta. He inspected the face of every fashionable dress that passed over the threshold, and was starting to think that he'd lost a guinea to a rather tricky servant when—there she was.

Just like the night he'd spied her at the theatre, Araminta was attired in a deep red, velvet gown. She led the way into the drawing room with her three sisters trailing behind her. She didn't glance his way as she passed by, but Grey found himself hard pressed to tear his gaze away from her. The assemblage quieted as the ladies greeted their hostess.

"By the way you've honed your eyes on her like a hound after the cunning fox, I assume that is the lady you are attempting to pursue?"

"It is," Grey returned. "The woman in green is your target."

He surveyed the lady for a moment and then said, "Indeed. I suppose we'll find out if I'm the crack shot you hope me to be."

Grey wished for that very thing as their hostess began to speak. After a brief introduction, she brought her daughter up to the seat of distinction. She was a perfect English rose with her creamy skin, bright blue eyes and curly blond hair that was pulled back from her face, a few ringlets left down to curl and dance about her shoulders. She must be a first season debutante, for she looked as though she was fresh out of the schoolroom.

As she began to read a story from E.T.A. Hoffman about "The Nutcracker and the Mouse King," he asked himself why he couldn't have been drawn to someone like her. Life would certainly be much easier if he had pursued her. In truth, he might have already secured a proposal. But the idea of wedding such a naïve young girl made his stomach churn. He'd always preferred women who were well seasoned and not so empty-headed. He wanted to enjoy an intelligent conversation and with these simpering young misses, it was nearly impossible to do so. Most of them were merely concerned with the latest fashions and their current needlework.

He shuddered at the idea he would be saddled with someone like that for the rest of his days. That was why he'd always preferred his peccadilloes and avoided entanglement—until that night at the theatre where one woman had suddenly brought him to heel with nothing more than her strong presence. And now that Lady Isadora stood between him and Lady Araminta, the challenge had become even more prominent.

But in the end, he vowed he would overcome any obstacle.

Restless, Grey forced himself to sit still throughout the reading, for it wouldn't be long until he would be in front of Araminta once again. And this time, he intended to do whatever was necessary to convince her to entertain his suit.

"HE'S *HERE*!" Calliope hissed in Araminta's ear as they had sat down and settled in for the reading.

"Who, dear?" Araminta pretended a sudden interest in fixing the lace on her dress, but she knew exactly whom her sister was referring to.

"Why the Earl of Somers, of course!" Calliope returned, as if it she was rather dimwitted. "Perhaps during intermission you should speak to him."

Araminta ground her teeth at being put in this precarious situation. Who would have even thought the earl would enjoy something as simple as a book reading? She'd actually accepted this invitation for exactly the reason that she thought she *wouldn't* see him there.

She fidgeted slightly, her temperature rising, for she could almost *feel* his gaze boring into her. Of course, that could just be her imagination. For all she knew he'd decided to heed her words and he was there for another reason. She glanced at Lady Journton's daughter who had just walked to the front of the room and wondered if perhaps he hadn't decided to move on to another conquest already. She studied the girl, trying to imagine Lord Somers pursing her, and found it highly unlikely. She was too innocent for the likes of him, although he was a known rake.

She frowned. Surely he wouldn't try to take advantage of her? Or lead her down the infamous Scandal Lane at Hyde Park? If so, then surely it was Araminta's duty to safeguard the girl from his clutches.

She sat up a bit straighter and forced herself to focus on the enchanting story about a little girl who traveled to the Land of Sweets with a Nutcracker Prince, where they have to fight off the evil Mouse King. She would have been thoroughly engrossed in the fairy tale if she hadn't been so distracted by the presence of the man sitting somewhere behind her.

As soon as the reading was over, the assemblage clapped and the girl's cheeks turned a becoming shade of pink as she offered a curtsy. As her mother announced that there would be refreshments served in the parlor, Araminta was grateful for the chance to move about and ease the sudden tension that was making her shoulders feel tight, although there was no doubt that she would be forced to encounter Lord Somers at some point.

It turned out she didn't have very long to wait at all. Before they had even made it out of the drawing room, Lord Somers smoothly stepped in her path. "Lady Araminta." He offered an elegant bow. As he greeted the rest of her sisters in turn, he addressed Livy. "Lady Olivia. I trust you are suffering no ill effects from your fall in the Thames."

"No, my lord," she returned quietly.

"I'm relieved to hear it." He offered a broad smile, which made Araminta's toes curl in her slippers. "I was hoping to present a dear friend of mine." As the man standing next to him stepped forward, Araminta noted that he was rather handsome with his russet hair and piercing hazel eyes. It also didn't escape her attention that his focus was directed on Isadora. *Interesting.*

"I can speak for myself, Somers," he said deeply. He reached out and grasped Isadora's gloved hand and brought it to his lips where he kissed her knuckles lightly. "Remington Fletcher, Marquess of Osgood."

"Lady Isadora Bevelstroke." Araminta lifted a brow at the breathless quality to her elder sister's voice. She was generally adept at keeping herself distanced from any sort of flattery, but there was apparently something different about the marquess.

"May I escort you to the parlor?" Osgood offered an arm to Isadora, and she readily accepted him. She slid a glance to Araminta, her cheeks coloring slightly as she was led away.

Calliope, ever the teasing sister, offered her services to Olivia. "Shall we depart?"

Olivia giggled as she threaded her arm through hers.

Once they were gone, that left Araminta alone with Lord Somers. He smiled almost sheepishly. "I suppose that leaves the two of us." He crooked his arm at her and she slipped her hand through his, resting her fingers lightly on his muscular forearm.

"Something tells me you did this on purpose," she murmured.

He put his other hand over his heart. "I'm wounded that you would believe I would stoop to such means just to get you alone, Lady Araminta. I'm a gentleman." Although the wink he offered her was full of deviltry.

"Hmm." Her lips twitched of their own volition as they found their way to the refreshment table. Glancing over the array of delights to be had, she passed them over while the earl popped a sweetmeat into his mouth.

She thought nothing further of the action until those blue eyes looked directly at her as he began to slowly lick each of his fingers in turn. A swirling warmth took over her midsection, and she was frozen to the spot, her eyes riveted on the action.

"Delicious," he murmured.

"Er...yes," she stammered in turn.

He reached out and plucked another candy from the silver platter. "Would you care for one?" He held it out to her and she realized that he intended to *feed* her in the presence of all of the other guests milling about.

Her face heated. "I don't think that would be appropriate."

"Why?" he challenged. "Don't tell me you're afraid."

Araminta clenched her fists at her sides. He was testing her resolve, so to prove how strong she was against his virility she obediently opened her mouth. He smiled wickedly as he set the treat directly on her tongue. Instantly, the sweet sensation flooded her mouth, and combined with the brush of his fingers along her tongue as he withdrew, she wasn't sure she could even swallow after that.

Thankfully, she managed to do so, if nothing else, than to spare herself the embarrassment that would have ensued if she'd coughed and sputtered.

As it slid down her throat, he leaned close and whispered in her ear, "If you found that delightful, I guarantee that I can do things to you that are *much* more enjoyable."

Araminta couldn't breathe. She suddenly wanted nothing more than to learn exactly what he meant. But she forced herself to blink and put her wayward fantasies back on track. "The painting." She cleared her throat and attempted to speak more forcefully. "I appreciate the sentiment, but it's entirely too intimate of a gift for me to accept."

"I'm afraid that's impossible, for it's the perfect complement to the one I have hanging in my bedchamber. It's entitled, 'Wanderer above the Sea of Fog.'" He paused. "It is, of course, how I see my future, one very similar to yours. But while you are anticipating the sunrise of a new day, I envision a lonely existence, staring out at the vast abandon."

"How very poetic, but decidedly untrue," she countered. "You are an earl. Surely any lady would be overjoyed at the prospect of becoming a countess."

He plucked another sweetmeat from the tray and popped it into his mouth. "Not every lady," he corrected.

Araminta wasn't sure how to respond to that, for it was nothing but the truth. She'd made her sentiments perfectly clear. He had only to accept them, but it was apparent with this conversation that he was still holding out hope she might change her mind.

She stood up straighter and told herself that she could get through this. She could withstand the earl's magnetic pull. As she glanced about the room, she spied Calliope and Olivia in a chat with a few other women, but as her focus shifted and she spied Isadora in a rather secluded corner with the marquess, irritation sparked. Isa had been the one who had reminded Araminta of her place, to remember the vow that they had made with their younger sisters. And yet, she was cavorting with Osgood in much the same manner as she herself had encouraged Lord Somers' attentions.

Araminta was surprised that the marquess had immediately shown such a strong interest in—

Abruptly, she turned her head to stare at the earl. "You *did* plan this!" she accused hotly.

He paused, but his expression looked rather sheepish. "I don't know what you mean," he hedged.

"Don't you?" She crossed her arms. "Osgood is here as a distraction for Isadora so you can continue flirting with me. Tell me I'm wrong."

He hesitated, as if weighing his options and then shrugged. "You're not wrong."

While she'd suspected his motives, she didn't think that he

would actually admit to them. "You are shameless! Is the marquess even trustworthy?"

He bristled at that. "I don't cavort with so many unsavory types as you might think. Osgood is a gentleman above reproach. He's a war hero and a close confidante to the Duke of Wellington." Some of her anger deflated as he continued. He moved toward her and lowered his voice so that they weren't overheard. "But how else was I supposed to convince you that my intentions toward you are sincere other than having some time alone with you to prove my adoration?"

He lifted a finger and trailed it down the side of her neck, causing her to shiver. "I know that if you would just lower your defenses for a short time, you would see that we could have a very harmonious union."

She ceased to breathe until he stepped back. But then she felt bereft without him. "I'll be at Hyde Park tonight at midnight if you are interested, waiting in my carriage on Scandal Lane." He lifted a brow. "I'm sure you've heard of it."

She narrowed her eyes. "You would *dare* to tarnish my reputation and trap me into marrying you?"

"No." He shook his head. "I'm merely giving you one last chance to trust me. If you don't appear, then I will know that any further hopes are truly in vain and I will bow away graciously, never to trouble you again. However—" His eyes heated. "If you do come, I will ensure that your efforts are worthwhile."

With that, he bowed and after one last lingering look at her, he walked away.

~

"You want to leave now?" Osgood blinked in confusion. "The reading isn't over."

"I accomplished what I came for," Grey returned. "Don't tell me you're that intrigued to find out what happens to the Nutcracker?"

The marquess rolled his eyes with a snort. "No. In truth, I was enjoying getting better acquainted with Lady Isadora."

Grey withheld a shudder as they gathered their outerwear and walked out into the brisk evening air. His breath formed a cloud as they descended the steps and walked toward his carriage. Even a few snowflakes had begun to fall. It looked like the perfect setting for a seduction, if the lady would only agree. "That dragon of a sister? Heaven save me."

Osgood lifted a brow. "I don't know what you mean. I found her to be rather agreeable."

"At least that's one of us," Grey muttered as they climbed inside his carriage. As they drove away from the Journton townhouse, his blood hummed with anticipation. He knew he'd piqued Lady Araminta's interest, even though she had done her best to hide it. But was it enough for her to make the short trek to Hyde Park that night?

Once he'd dropped Osgood off at White's where he spent the majority of his time, instead of taking him home, Grey instructed his driver to go to the one place he generally avoided, unless it was around the holidays when his mother expected his presence.

As he walked up the steps to his sister's townhouse, he rapped on the door. After a moment, the Montrose butler opened it. If Grey didn't know better he might have thought he looked a bit worse for wear. But trying to manage a household with nine children under the same roof was likely quite an undertaking.

"Lord Somers." He bowed and moved to the side, giving him more room to enter. "May I take your outerwear?"

As Grey handed over his coat, hat and gloves, he asked, "Where might I find my sister?"

"I believe she is upstairs in her private sitting room with her youngest child, my lord."

"Very good." Grey inclined his head and walked to the second floor where his sister's chamber was located. Although she had her own suite of rooms apart from her husband, it was apparent by their brood of children that they were never far apart for long.

He knocked softly on the door and waited. After a moment, a familiar feminine voice bade him to enter. When he walked inside, he saw Melinda reclining on a chaise and holding a blanket wrapped bundle in her arms, a tuft of downy dark hair peeking over the edge. When she spied him, her eyes lit up, even if her brow furrowed in apparent confusion. "Grey! While I don't know the reason for this impromptu visit, I daresay I'm glad for it."

He smiled. There wasn't a time when Melinda hadn't been overjoyed to see him, but then, they had always been rather close during their childhood. "I thought it was time I met my latest niece." She moved her legs, giving him room to sit beside her, which he did.

"I should say so," she chided gently. "Mary is already two weeks old."

"Precisely. I didn't want to rush your recovery time, nor intrude on you and Eli when you are getting acquainted with your latest blessing."

She looked at him pointedly. "You never intrude, Grey. You're family." With that, she handed the baby over to him.

He knew he should be used to holding a baby in his arms by now. After all, he'd held all eight of Melinda's others before this one, but each time he looked into that small face with that button nose and small cupid's bow mouth he was struck anew by how delicate new life was. And how very precious.

The child was sleeping, but he couldn't resist whispering, "Hallo, Mary. I'm your Uncle Grey."

There was no change to the expression as the baby slept on rather soundly, although she did move slightly as if acknowledging his presence.

"It's rather late to be calling," his sister noted. "Not that I'm complaining, but I just assumed you would be out roaming the town with Lord Blakely as usual."

It was true he hadn't seen Sebastian for a couple of days, but whenever the subject of matrimony was broached anywhere near his friend, he tended to find a way to hide. "He's still around, but our pursuits have turned to different matters of late."

Melinda gasped. "Does this mean that you've finally decided to marry?"

Grey chuckled at the hope that laced her voice. "I've considered it, yes."

She clasped her hands together. "I told Eli that you weren't without redemption!"

Again, he laughed. He was rather certain that what he was feeling for Lady Araminta had nothing to do with that.

"Do you have a special lady in mind?" she prodded.

"I do. However, it's the attempt of convincing her of the same that I find difficult to surmount."

She frowned. "That can't be true. You're a wealthy earl and as such, quite a catch. Who wouldn't be eager to become a countess?"

Who, indeed, he thought wryly. "Apparently, that would be Lady Araminta Bevelstroke."

"Bevelstroke." She considered the name for a moment, and then her eyes widened slightly. "You don't mean she's one of the late Duke of Marlington's daughters?"

"She is." His lips twitched. "Although I'm surprised you know of them, as they have only recently arrived in town."

"Of course I know them. The scandal rags have been full of speculation. Not only that, but they claim they wish to be 'independent.'" She said the last as if it was quite unthinkable.

"That much is true," Grey concurred. "It's been one of the reasons I've had some difficulty courting her."

She eyed him steadily for a moment then said, "You truly care for her, don't you?"

"I've grown fond of her, yes." That was as far as he was willing to commit when it came to how he felt for Araminta. In truth, he wasn't sure he could put all of these swirling emotions into words.

She grasped his arm. "Then you mustn't let her get away. You have to find a way to win her over."

And yet, that was the crux of the matter, and one of the reasons he'd come to see Melinda tonight, for some much needed advice into the mind of the opposite sex. "I daresay I've been trying to do just that, but she's rather adamant in her desire to remain unattached. How can I convince her otherwise?"

"Simple." She shrugged. "You must seduce her."

Grey snorted. "And here I thought you might have given me a reasonable answer."

"It *is* reasonable." Her cheeks colored suddenly. "How do you imagine I fell in love with Eli so quickly? I was quite enamored of his kisses."

"I can see I'm going to have to have a firm chat with my brother-in-law," Grey muttered.

She laughed. "I think it's a little late for that, don't you?" She gestured to the baby he held. She lifted Mary out of his arms and said, "Now, go, and win the heart of your fair maiden."

He rolled his eyes. "Shall I take my broadsword and chain mail?"

Grey rose and bent to kiss his sister's cheek. "Thank you."

As he straightened, the door opened and his brother-in-law strode in with a wide, welcoming smile. "I heard that you were here. I apologize for not greeting you earlier. I was in my study taking care of some business."

Grey eyed the dark-haired man in a new light than before. With his spectacles and kind demeanor, he couldn't imagine that he would have defiled his sister before they were wed. He started to do the math regarding when their eldest child was born and wondered if perhaps...

"Montrose," Grey returned evenly, suddenly skeptical of the man standing before him.

Eli frowned curiously, but otherwise, he said nothing as he walked over and laid a gentle hand on his wife's shoulder, peering down at their latest creation. In that moment, with the absolute love and adoration shining from his eyes that was mirrored in Melinda's expression, Grey decided that whatever Eli had done to secure his sister's hand had been worth it in the end, for they were happily in love.

He could only wish for the same ending with Araminta.

Grey quietly left the room.

CHAPTER 8

Araminta's mind was whirling with every minute that ticked passed on the ormolu clock on the mantel in her bedchamber. She knew what would happen if she met Lord Somers that evening—and that she would lose him if she didn't.

He'd given her the choice.

The question that remained was what was she going to do?

She'd seen him depart with Osgood during intermission, and as she resumed her seat with her sisters to hear what had happened to the Nutcracker, Araminta realized that she hadn't allowed a single word to penetrate her brain, although she had clapped along with the rest of the assemblage when it was over.

On the way back to their house, she saw that she wasn't the only one reticent to join in Calliope and Olivia's conversation regarding the entertainment. Isadora said little during the ride, and excused herself the moment they returned home. Araminta could only guess that she had been rather charmed by Osgood's attentions, and when they were stripped away, she was feeling rather bereft. For as much as they all prided themselves on being women who wanted to live independently from a man, when a member from the opposite sex noticed a lady and showered her with attention, it was hard to remain unaffected. Females had their pride too.

But while she didn't imagine that the marquess' affections could be sincere, especially when Araminta figured out that Lord Somers had convinced him to attend the reading in order to distract Isa, the earl had told Araminta more than once that he wished to further their courtship.

But how could she believe that to be true? They had only shared a handful of interactions. What had made Lord Somers so determined that he should have *her* as his wife?

Araminta sat down on the edge of her four poster bed and put a hand to her pounding head as the clock chimed the hour of eleven. She was already dressed for bed, having dismissed her maid some time ago, so there was no reason for her not to already be under the covers, her eyes shut and starting to fall into dreamland.

And yet…

She couldn't help but glance outside at the softly falling snow and imagine the earl sitting inside of his carriage, waiting to see if she would arrive, wondering if she would join him so that they might allow Scandal Lane to live up to its torrid reputation.

She saw his face in her mind, the black hair and those piercing blue eyes. She imagined his hands touching her bare skin as his lips found hers…

Stop it! She stood up and threw back the covers of the bed, determined to ignore the yearning in her heart that dared her to break all the rules. She climbed underneath the coverlet and pulled it up to her chin, laying her arms over the top on either side, as if trying to pin herself in place.

She adjusted her head on the pillow, but try as she might she did nothing more than stare at the ceiling above her. She squeezed her eyes shut and imagined the field full of white puffy sheep as they grazed on the grass near her father's estate. Her throat thickened suddenly, as her mind took her back to her childhood, for she craved those carefree days when he had been alive.

She still mourned his loss, but she kept those tears to herself in private, not wishing to upset her sisters. It had been bad enough when they had to pack up and leave the estate to some unknown heir that would eventually move in with his family. While Araminta and her siblings knew each wooden board that creaked, and that one of the portraits of their ancestors that lined the gallery was never perfectly straight, no matter what they did to correct the problem, and the library had over one thousand volumes, it didn't matter, because it was no longer their home.

Perhaps that's why her mind was making her consider the earl's proposal, because deep down, she wanted that sort of life again. She missed confiding in her father and the comforting hug he would give her when she was upset. But she didn't want to distance herself from her sisters by going back on her word. To lose their trust would be to lose…what was left.

What the earl offered was a fantasy, a fairy tale, for they might decide to be happy for a time, but what happened when tragedy struck? Her father had buried four wives, all of which he claimed to care for deeply. Could she endure such heartache?

Or perhaps they both lived a long life together. Would it be fraught with strife once the excitement wore off? Dare she take a gamble on such a risky endeavor?

She rolled onto her side and put her hands beneath her cheek.

She wasn't leaving this room. She wasn't going to think about him any further, and when the dawn came, she would be grateful that she'd made the rational decision to stay right where she was.

The clock chimed the half hour. Eleven-thirty. She clenched her jaw and blotted out the image of him waiting in his carriage, waiting for her…

SHE WASN'T COMING.

Grey could feel it in his bones, and yet, he couldn't yet tell the carriage driver to take him home. He didn't want to concede defeat, that he hadn't been enough of a temptation for Lady Araminta to ease the strictures she'd placed upon herself. He didn't want to admit that she wasn't willing to take a chance on him, so that he might prove that they could have a rather satisfying life together.

So here he sat, parked on the infamous Scandal Lane and feeling more foolish with each passing moment.

He shoved a hand through his hair and realized that it must be well after midnight by now. If Sebastian were here, he'd likely have a good laugh at the merry chase Grey had set for himself. "Why don't we go have a drink and drown the loss of your pride, old friend?" He could hear his mocking voice even now.

He gritted his teeth together. There were plenty of eligible ladies in the ton who would eagerly accept his attentions. He should turn his focus toward one of them if he was set on finally setting up his nursery. But then, he hadn't even known he wanted to marry until he'd looked across the theatre and saw the woman in red. If he couldn't win over Araminta, then he would concede defeat graciously and likely turn back to his bachelor ways.

He leaned his head back against the seat and decided he would give her five more minutes to appear. After that, he would honor his vow to bow out.

The sound of a carriage pulling to a halt outside caused him to sit back up. He opened the door to his coach and his heart began pumping wildly when he saw a cloaked figure descend from a hired hackney. He knew it was her even before she turned her head and her lovely face come into view.

She said nothing as she came forward, although the hired hackney remained where it was. "Lady Araminta," he murmured softly when she paused before him. He held out a hand to her and she accepted it as she climbed into the carriage with him.

She sat on the opposite seat from him and before he could say anything, she spoke. "This doesn't mean that I accept your proposal."

He inclined his head. "I see."

"I was lying in bed, telling myself all the reasons why I should stay there." She glanced up at him with those enchanting gray eyes. "But I kept picturing you sitting here all alone and I realized I couldn't do that to you. You have paid me the highest compliment in your pursuit for my hand so I felt I owed it to you to come here and talk."

He watched her intently, but said nothing as she continued.

She returned her gaze back to her clasped hands in her lap. "You see, I made a vow to my sisters that I cannot break. I promised that I would be there for them under any circumstances. If I were to marry you, then it would erase their trust in me." She took a deep breath. "So I am here to offer a proposal of my own." She lifted her eyes once more.

He lifted a brow, intrigued. "And that would be?"

"While a union between us may not be possible, I have always been… curious about what happens between a man and a woman in the…bedchamber."

Grey stilled, but didn't dare speak.

"So, if you are willing," she continued matter-of-fact, as if they were speaking of something as inconsequential as the weather. "I'm offering a brief affair for one night only. I firmly believe that what you feel toward me is mere physical attraction and if you purge yourself of me, then your desire will be satiated. You will have what you want and I will have kept my word to my sisters, while enjoying that which shall be denied to me in the future as an independent lady." She visibly swallowed. "Do you agree to my terms?"

Grey admired her boldness as well as her devotion to her siblings. Both qualities weren't often found among the debutantes he'd encountered in London. But then, Araminta was a grown woman of six and twenty. She was old enough to know what she wanted and that was him, although perhaps not as fully as he would wish. But at least it was a start. And if it came to pass that a single night of passion was all they would share, then he supposed it would have to be enough.

"If we do this," he began. "When would you like this…event to take place?"

She considered for a moment and then said, "Next Friday."

He lifted his brows. "That's Christmas Eve, the night of the Gravesend ball."

"It is," she agreed. "But what better time to embark on such a magical night?"

He inclined his head. "Indeed. I shall make the arrangements to ensure it's not one to forget."

Her cheeks flushed adoringly, and then she said, "I suppose that's it then."

She reached for the handle of the carriage to depart, but he stopped her with a hand on her arm. "Don't you think a demonstration of what you can expect is in order?"

She hesitated, stilling completely, but then she slowly nodded.

He pulled her back to him, situating her where she straddled his lap, her knees resting on either side of him. He gently pushed the hood of her cloak back to reveal her dark hair falling around her shoulders. It was the first time he'd seen it unbound, and the sight stirred his blood even more than the most practiced courtesan. He slipped his hand into those silken locks and urged her forward to meet his waiting mouth.

IT HADN'T BEEN Araminta's first kiss, but it was the only one she would ever remember henceforth. While a couple of eager village boys had attempted to coax her with their attentions when she'd been younger, she had easily rebuffed their advances. It was clear that they had been terribly inexperienced, for the way Lord Somers kissed her was nothing short of...*enthralling*. His mouth moved across hers with a knowledge born of practice and she could tell that he'd had plenty of it.

When his hand slowly lowered to brush the underside of her breast, she gasped. She'd left the house on an impulse, but it wasn't as though she would have called for her maid to assist her into her stays. She'd thought that her chemise, gown, and cloak would have been enough for a quick escapade, but now she realized how dangerous that had been, for as he slipped a hand beneath her cloak and cupped her through her gown, toying with the taunt nipple, she didn't want the sweet torture to stop.

She'd waited years for this and she found that she didn't want to wait any longer. What if something happened and she couldn't meet him on Christmas Eve? She might never have the chance to experience such passion ever again.

"Grey, please. I don't want this to be over yet." It was the first time she'd dared to use his Christian name, but she prayed he would sense the urgency in her voice.

He drew back to look into her eyes. "It's not Christmas Eve," he said huskily and she knew that he was just as affected as she was.

"I don't care. I changed my mind. I want this and I want you. *Now*."

She could tell that he wavered. "You should have a bed and roses and candlelight—"

She put her hands on his rough cheeks with a slight hint of stubble. "That doesn't matter to me. I only want to *feel*."

He hesitated for a moment longer and then he kissed her with even more heat than before. His tongue swept inside of her mouth, and she moaned at the slick sensation. When he delved beneath her skirts and began to stroke the aching bud between her thighs in the same manner, she gasped at the intensity. Above and below, it was all beginning to turn to molten fire that spread throughout her limbs, until she gave a muffled cry against his lips and burst apart.

While she was still coming down from the heavens, he reached between them and undid his trousers, freeing his engorged manhood. With one last look at her, both of them panting heavily, he seemed to be waiting for her final consent.

"Yes." It was all she had to utter for him to lift her hips slightly and set her on top of him. She tensed slightly at the intrusion, but when he began to fondle her breasts once more, kissing the side of her neck, she was soon lost to the pleasure and relaxed.

He eased inside of her, inch by glorious inch until he thrust upward and entered her fully. She bit his shoulder at the sudden sting, but it quickly faded as he began a rhythm that had her wrapping her arms around him. By the time he found his release, she was sobbing his name as she crested once more.

As he went still, Araminta shut her eyes tightly. She wasn't sure what to say, or if words were even needed in this moment.

He pulled back and pushed her chin upward with his knuckles. "Look at me, Araminta."

She lifted her lids and gazed into his handsome face. In that moment she knew that, whatever else she did in this life, she'd made the right choice by giving herself to him.

"I know you still don't want to marry me, but I hope that someday I can convince you to change your mind." He smiled. "For the second time."

She smiled. "Let's just content ourselves with this moment right now and leave tomorrow where it belongs."

He reluctantly nodded his head, and she slipped off his lap. As he put himself to rights and fastened his trousers, she pulled the hood of her cloak back over her hair.

Before she departed, he grasped her hand and kissed the backs of her knuckles. "I hope that I can still see you on Christmas Eve."

"You will," she returned evenly. "If you attend the Gravesend ball."

Araminta returned to the hackney that had waited for her return, and although the driver didn't smirk, she had the feeling he knew what had just happened. Her cheeks burned with sudden embarrassment as she instructed him to drive her home.

He dropped her off in the mews behind the house and she let herself in through the servants' entrance near the kitchens, the same way she'd taken her leave.

However, the moment she shut the door behind her and shoved her cloak back, a light flared to life in the room. "I wondered if you were coming back tonight."

Araminta put a hand to her pounding heart at the sight of Isadora sitting in her nightdress and robe at the simple table, her dark hair in a simple plait falling over her shoulder. But it was her eyes, that condemning expression on her face that made Araminta bristle. "I wasn't aware that I had to answer to you. I am a woman grown, am I not?"

"Indeed. Which is why I wish you would start acting like it, rather than some tart who must sneak out for a late night tryst."

Araminta gasped. She'd never heard her sister speak like that to her. It hurt, but more than that, it infuriated her. "What I do isn't your concern."

"Isn't it?" Isadora countered with a raised brow, as she stood and walked around the table to confront her directly. "If you are caught cavorting with your lover, your sordid reputation not only affects you, but the rest of us. Would you condemn Callie and Livy? We came to London to start a new chapter in our lives as independent women, not for you to have the chance to spread your legs for the first handsome earl to stroll along."

Araminta's hand flew out before she could think better of it, and she struck Isadora across the cheek. The sharp contact resounded throughout the otherwise silent room. "How *dare* you!" she hissed. "You are not speaking to me as though you are a concerned sister, but someone who is jealous. I'm sorry that Lord Osgood didn't pay any further addresses to you, but that is no reason to lash out at me!"

Instead of being offended, Isadora laughed. "Oh, that's rich, Minty! Always tossing your mistakes back in my face. It's been like that since we were girls. Why did I think it would ever change?"

Araminta narrowed her eyes. "Then perhaps I should just find alternate lodgings and ensure that you never have to set eyes upon me again." With that, she left Isadora to stare at her retreating back as she headed upstairs to her chamber.

However, the moment the door shut behind her, the frustrating tears that she'd held back started to stream down her face. After such a remarkable night with Lord Somers, she'd had to come home to endure Isadora's harsh criticism. And while she felt her elder sister was being rather unforgiving, much of what she had said was true.

What if she'd been caught on Scandal Lane tonight? It was true that the shame wouldn't just fall on her, but on all of them as well. She'd made an error in judgment, allowing her fascination for the earl to take over her common sense, but she was starting to believe that what was happening between them wasn't just a passing fancy.

In truth, she feared she was falling in love with him.

She wiped angrily at her tears. But it wasn't as if she could suddenly alter her plans and wish for something other than the independence she had once craved. However, the idea of settling down and having her own household and becoming a mother, raising a brood of children was turning out to be just as appealing.

So then why was she feeling so guilty?

CHAPTER 9

The next morning, after soaking in the bath until the water had cooled considerably, Araminta went downstairs long after breakfast. She had thought that, by now, Isadora might have gone out to take her daily walk. With her eyes still slightly red and puffy from her crying episode the night before, she didn't want her sister's knowing face to be the first thing she saw.

A glance out the window revealed the snow was coming down rather heavily. She entered the parlor and picked up the latest edition of the *Times.* When she'd told Isadora that she would start looking for alternate lodgings, she had been serious. While Callie and Livy would likely wonder at her reasons for it, she intended to be as vague as possible. She might be on the outs with Isadora, but there was no reason to concern her younger sisters.

As if on cue, Calliope took that moment to sail into the parlor. "It's about time you got up." She sat down next to her on the settee. "You're turning into a regular slugabed."

"I wasn't feeling well this morning," she hedged and hoped

that Callie would take the hint that she wasn't in a talkative mood.

She didn't. With a frown she asked, "What are you doing perusing the paper? I thought you hated gossip?"

"That's not what I'm looking for." She hesitated, but since it wouldn't be a surprise when she moved out, she added, "I'm thinking of getting my own lodgings."

Calliope blinked. "What? Why?"

She shrugged. "I just think it's time."

"But I thought we were going to be independent women together?"

Araminta slide a gaze toward her. "That's not really the definition of 'independent,' now is it?"

Instead of finding the irony, Calliope shot to her feet. Her fists were clenched at her sides, her irritation obvious. "I don't know what has gotten into you lately, but while you feel the sudden need to desert us all, rest assured that *I* won't do the same."

She stormed out of the room and Araminta sighed heavily upon her departure. She wasn't going to speak ill of Isadora, nor tell her younger sisters the real reason she was looking to move forward on her own. Last night's confrontation was between her and Isa and that was how it would remain.

A short time later, Araminta gathered her outerwear, prepared to head out into the snow that was still coming down rather heavily, when Isadora spied her in the foyer. She paused and, for a moment, looked as though she wasn't sure what to say. Finally, she asked, "Where can you possibly be going in this weather?"

By the censure in her tone, Isa likely assumed Araminta was going to see Lord Somers. As she drew on her gloves, she said in a matter-of-fact tone, "I've found a ladies' boarding house that is looking for renters. I thought to check it out to see if it's reputable."

"I see." Isadora's expression hadn't changed; it was still as unyielding as it had been the night before.

She turned to go, but Isadora found her voice once more. "So you're serious about leaving?"

Araminta paused. "I told you that last night when we discussed my… nocturnal activities." She lifted a brow in challenge. "It seems to be for the best, don't you think? I should hate to bring shame and scandal down on this house because I dared entertain thoughts of a man."

Isadora frowned. "I may have spoken in haste last night. I was angry and—"

Araminta waved a hand. "It doesn't matter. All is forgiven, but I must go. The carriage is waiting."

With that, she strode out the front door without looking back.

~

"My lord?"

Grey snapped to attention as the butler looked at him expectantly. "Er, yes. That's fine."

The servant nodded almost uncertainly as he took his leave and Grey wondered what he'd just agreed to. He was in his study attempting to work on some estate ledgers, but he found his thoughts were sadly distracted by the memory of Lady Araminta. He'd wanted to call upon her that morning, but he'd forced himself to refrain. He actually wasn't quite sure how to approach her just yet. Nor was he prepared to deal with her sister's wrath when he pleaded his case of matrimony.

He reached into his pocket and pulled out a small box. He opened it to reveal his grandmother's engagement ring. He held it up to the light coming in through the window. Even though it was snowing quite heavily outside and the sky was covered with gray clouds, the ring still sparkled with a certain brilliance. It was a lovely amber setting within a circle of diamonds. He remembered quite fondly his grandmother wearing the ring as well as the day she'd given it to him with the promise that he should only give it to the woman who had taken his heart. He never thought this day would actually come, but then he hadn't ever met a woman like Lady Araminta Bevelstroke before now.

He didn't care how long it took, or what he had to do to convince her to choose him as her husband, he only knew that he was determined not to take no for an answer.

"My lord?"

Grey sighed as he tucked the ring back in its box and tucked it within the secure pocket of his jacket. "I thought I made it clear I didn't wish to be disturbed."

The butler didn't even have a chance to reply as a feminine voice intruded. "Perhaps the earl might make an exception for me."

Grey's interest was instantly piqued as Lady Isadora stood in the doorframe. He stood as he waved the servant away. "I will always make time for such a lovely lady," he said smoothly.

The door was closed as Lady Isadora strode forward. She offered a brief curtsy as Grey motioned to the chair opposite his large oak desk. As she sat down, he did the same. Threading his hands before him on the top, he asked, "What can I do for you, my lady?"

She hadn't removed her cloak, gloves or bonnet, so Grey assumed she didn't intend to stay long. "I know Araminta snuck out to see you last night."

His brow furrowed slightly. He was afraid something like that might happen. "I see."

"No, I don't think you do," she countered. She placed her hands delicately in her lap. "I said some harsh words to her last night, and now she has her mind made up to move out. What I want to know is if your attentions toward her are sincere or if you look at her as just another dalliance."

Grey thought of the ring in his pocket. "I can assure you that I have asked Araminta, on numerous occasions, to marry me. She has declined every time because of her devotion to you and her younger sisters."

"Indeed." Isadora smiled almost sadly. "I had the feeling that when we ventured to London that our time together would be short lived, but I knew we would eventually go our separate ways, wherever that might take us." She eyed him steadily. "I think that you will make a fine match for her. Your holdings appear to be sound, and your annual income is quite substantial. And as long as you truly care for her, then you have my blessing."

Grey was rather overjoyed to hear that he had finally won her over, although he couldn't help but smirk when she spoke of his finances. "I take it you have been checking up on me?"

"I wouldn't be a very good businesswoman, intent on living independently if I didn't look into every investment that was presented to me," she countered. "Including those involving a union with someone in my family."

She got to her feet, and Grey followed suit. He held out his hand to her. "I have no doubt you will succeed in whatever you choose to do, Lady Isadora."

She hesitated a moment and then reached out and shook his hand. "And I believe that you will make my sister very happy." As they parted, she added, "Might I suggest announcing your engagement at the Gravesend ball on Christmas Eve?"

While Grey had Isadora's approval, he had yet to fully win over Araminta. "Are you sure she will accept my hand this time?"

Isadora's lips curved upward in what could only be called a devilish smile. "I have an idea about that…"

ARAMINTA GENTLY TOUCHED the hem of the bright red gown she was wearing. It was the same one she'd worn to the opera the night she'd met Lord Somers, but Isadora had said it was the "perfect" dress to wear to the Gravesend ball that night. It didn't matter that the very sight of it caused a burning ache of longing in her chest. Or that, starting tomorrow, she would be moving into the boarding house where she would truly be alone. Most of her things were already packed and waiting by the foyer.

Calliope had refused to speak to her for several days, but she'd finally softened toward her and the tension between them had eased somewhat. Isadora had also begun to treat her with more respect, to the point they had begun to laugh together once more. However, Olivia was the one she was most concerned about, for since her unfortunate fall through the freezing Thames, she'd been more withdrawn than usual.

When she'd learned of Araminta's plans to leave the townhouse, she'd hardly batted an eyelash, and now she claimed she had a headache and refused to attend the Gravesend ball, when Araminta and Isadora had high hopes that Olivia would find particular favor with the reticent, Duke of Gravesend, who had saved her life that fateful day. Unfortunately, Araminta decided that their matchmaking skills would have to be put on hold and finally gave in to her pleas to remain behind.

Araminta took one last look around the bedchamber that had become her new haven over the past few weeks, ever since they had chosen to leave their father's former estate and embark on an exciting new venture to London.

Little had she known what had awaited *her*.

With a deep breath, she headed downstairs, her hand trailing the bannister. Isadora and Calliope were already there, waiting patiently for her to join them.

Without a word, they walked outside together, one last united front as the Bevelstroke sisters, and Araminta's eyes stung with emotional tears. However, she blinked them away and focused on trying to enjoy the evening ahead.

The Gravesend townhouse was located in London on the other side of the square, but since it was snowing again this evening and it wouldn't be fashionable to arrive with a wet hem, nor without a proper conveyance to let them out at the front door, they took the carriage.

Once they finally entered the impressive, stately townhouse, they handed over their outerwear to one of the several footmen waiting and sought out their hostess. The Duchess of Gravesend looked quite similar to her dark-haired son, although her coiffure was threaded with silver and her demeanor was as elegant as Araminta would have imagined.

As Araminta approached her and they were introduced to the lady, the duchess' green eyes lit up with recognition. "Ah, yes. I hope your sister suffers no ill effects from her fall through the ice?" she asked kindly, her expression sincere.

"She is quite well, thank you for asking," Isadora replied. "However, Olivia was suffering a megrim and couldn't join us this evening."

The lady smiled almost sadly. "I was hoping my son, Miles, might attend the ball this evening, but he has chosen to retire to the country for the holiday season." She blinked and her melancholy eased, as if she suddenly remembered her place. "I hope you all have a wonderful time and if you need anything, any one of the servants will be glad to attend to you."

As they moved away and began to descend the steps into the ballroom, Calliope whispered, "What a rather depressing Christmas season it must be for her, to be abandoned by her own son?"

"We don't know his reasons, nor his circumstances, Callie," Isadora chided. "Don't be so quick to judge."

As her sisters walked ahead of her, Araminta took a moment to glance out over the crowd assembled below. With an array of evergreen branches and candles set about the large, elegant room, she could tell that the duchess had ensured the Christmas spirit was evident. Combined with the floor-length windows along one wall with their gilt-edged trim and the swirling marble floor at her feet, it was more than Araminta could have hoped for when it came to her first, official London ball.

As the orchestra began to tune their instruments on an alcove set apart from the guests, Araminta's throat began to tighten. She realized that the only thing missing from such a magical evening was a certain gentleman. She'd noticed more than one interested male guest glancing their direction, but unfortunately, Lord Somers was not among them.

Of course, what had she been expecting? She'd declined his proposals more than once and told him on numerous occasions to leave her alone. While Araminta loved her sisters dearly, she realized she'd made a terrible mistake in pushing the earl away. Her chest had ached with a terrible loss ever since she'd given herself to him that night nearly two weeks ago.

If only she could go back and do it all over again, she would have never gotten out of that carriage. Instead of coming home and facing Isadora's wrath and her own guilt, she should have confronted her siblings the next morning with Grey at her side.

With a sigh, she pushed those regrets out of her mind. There was no use lamenting what was already done. All she could do now was hold on to his memory.

As Isadora and Calliope were instantly whisked away to dance, Araminta declined the first few offers she was given. While decorum insisted that she couldn't stand up with anyone else that evening, she found that she wasn't really in the mood to waltz anyway. In truth, she was starting to think that she should have just remained behind with Olivia.

She wandered over to the refreshment table and accepted a glass of punch. After that, she headed to a secluded alcove and began to sip her drink. She watched the dancers swirling before her for a time and then quickly lost interest. She set aside her glass and headed down the hall toward the ladies' retiring room.

However, the moment she passed a darkened room on the way, the door opened and her arm was caught in a tight grip as she was pulled inside. She didn't have time to do more than gasp before a blindfold was placed over her eyes and a gag was placed in her mouth, her arms tied together in front of her.

Fear instantly shot through her as she was thrown over a firm, broad shoulder, and was too much in shock to react at first. She could feel her hair escaping its pins as she bounced against her captor's muscular back. As the cold air from outside struck her, she shivered. It was enough to wake up her senses. Since she couldn't scream in spite of the gag, she began to pound her bound fists against the man's torso and kick her feet in an attempt to get away.

His hold tightened as he swatted her backside. Again, shock kept her immobile until she found herself tossed inside of a carriage. As it set into motion, there was a rap on the roof and they began to roll forward.

She cursed, using every name she could think of to insult her captor, but they fell on deaf ears since they merely came out as a muffled distortion.

The chuckle that resounded from the opposite side was deep and rather… sensual in nature. It only infuriated her even more that he was taking pleasure in her upset. She kicked out her leg and was disappointed when it only came into contact with the seat. In the next moment, she found herself deposited on a decidedly firm lap, her bound arms tossed around his head.

He made a *tsk*ing sound and then dared to slide his hand underneath her skirts. She instantly tried to lash out, but he kept her immobile against that warm, firm chest. When he dared to touch that area she'd only reserved for one man, she jerked and tried to pull away from him. But as his deft fingers began to stroke her, her limbs grew heavy and she started to melt into the embrace.

As her breathing became labored, he removed her gag, presumably with his teeth, since his other hand was wrapped securely around her waist. "Please, don't do this," she sobbed, even as her traitorous body cried out for him to continue.

"I can't help but touch you, my love."

As he spoke, Araminta recognized that voice. "Grey?" she breathed. "What—?"

"Shh. Just relax and let me pleasure you."

It didn't take long until she reached her climax, knowing now that she was with the man she loved. As her body hummed in the aftermath, he removed his hand from beneath her skirts, as well as the blindfold from around her eyes.

When her gaze lit on that handsome face, she shook her head. "Was all of this truly necessary?"

"It was if I didn't want you to refuse me again," he replied with a soft smile. "To be honest, it was Isadora's idea. She knew this was the only way for me to convince you that we are meant to be together."

As her mind tried to process what he'd just said, she frowned. "I don't believe she said that. She has given me grief for being with you ever since the night I returned home from Scandal Lane." Her cheeks colored at the memory, along with what they'd just done.

"She said you would say that, which is why she told me to give you this." He reached into his jacket and pulled out a sealed letter.

Araminta took it from his grasp with trembling fingers. She broke the wax seal and opened it to find her sister's handwriting, strong and true as always.

My dear Minty,

. . .

If you are reading this, then the earl has succeeded in spiriting you away from the Gravesend ball, in true heroic fashion. Don't be angry at him, for it was my idea that he should abduct you. I knew you would be too devoted to all of us to go with him willingly. At least, at first. I hope that you have changed your mind about marrying him, as I believe he will treat you as you deserve.

Sometimes life doesn't always go the way we plan, but I believe this is the right path for you. And you were right. Perhaps I was a bit jealous that you have found a love worth holding on to. I should wish the same for Calliope and Olivia should they desire such. It was wrong of me to make you feel guilty or hold you back, acting as though you were abandoning us. I abandoned you for not trusting in your judgment, and for that I apologize.

Don't worry about us, for we intend to enjoy all of the delights London has to offer. As for you, my dear sister, allow the love you've been holding back to envelope you in its warmth. But most of all, be happy.

With sisterly affection,

Isa

Tears fell from Araminta's eyes as she held her sister's letter close to her heart.

"Is everything all right?"

She nodded her head and sniffed. "Everything is perfect." She laid a hand on his cheek. "She has given us her blessing."

"Indeed, she has," he agreed with a heart-stopping grin. "Which is why I instructed my driver to take us to Gretna Green where we can elope in true scandalous fashion."

She laughed, feeling lighter than she had in days. Or, if she was truly honest with herself, ever since their father had died and she had left his estate. With Grey she felt as though she was… home.

“I love you, Greyson Hartfield.”

His blue eyes shone with adoration. “And I love you, soon-to-be Araminta Hartfield, the Countess of Somers.”

She smiled broadly through her emotion and they kissed to celebrate their future.

AFTERWORD

I'd like to thank you for purchasing this book. I know you could have chosen any number of stories to read, but you picked this one and for that I am humbled and grateful! I hope that the romance captured your heart and added a smile to your day. If so, it would be awesome if you could share this book with your friends and family and post a review! Your feedback and support will help improve my writing and help me to continue growing as an author.

ABOUT THE AUTHOR

Tabetha Waite began her writing journey at a young age. At nine years old, she was crafting stories of all kinds on an old Underwood typewriter. She started reading romance in high school and immediately fell in love with the genre. She gained her first publishing contract with Etopia Press/Wolf Hill Publishing and released her debut novel in July of 2016 - "Why the Earl is After the Girl," the first book in her Ways of Love historical romance series. Since then, she has become a hybrid author, published with both Soul Mate and Radish Fiction, as well as transitioning into Indie publishing. She has won several awards for her books.

She is a small town, Missouri girl who continues to make her home in the Midwest with her husband and two wonderful daughters. When she's not writing novels filled with adventure and heart, she is either reading, or searching the local antique mall or flea market for the latest interesting find. You can find her on most any social media site, and she encourages fans of her work to join her mailing list for updates.

https://authortabethawaite.wix.com/romance

www.ingramcontent.com/pod-product-compliance
Ingram Content Group UK Ltd.
Pitfield, Milton Keynes, MK11 3LW, UK
UKHW040021200726
13854UKWH00001B/294

9 798422 149308